1.50

In the Hands of Outlaws

"If you know what's good for you, you'll put your arms around here and stand still while I tie you up."

Longarm had heard the chill of death in the adversary's voice too many times not to recognize it when Caspar spoke. He held his arms behind his back while the outlaw looped the leather strip around his wrists and tied it.

"That's better," Barnes said. "I don't see but one thing we can do with him, do you?"

Shaking his head, Caspar replied, "Nope. We'll have to get rid of him, and I won't mind doing the job. You want me to take care of it now?"

"No, damn it!" Barnes exclaimed. "I don't know the first thing about any of those men y̶͟_____ do you think would happen if one of _____ and began bragging about how they h̶____ arm away?"

Longarm was quick to grasp the oper_____ given him. In a quietly assured voice ____ two know what's good for you, you'____ free and give up."

"Like hell we will!" Caspar told hi____ going to be alive long enough to se____ up..."

TABOR EVANS

LONGARM

IN A DESERT SHOWDOWN

J

JOVE BOOKS, NEW YORK

LONGARM IN A DESERT SHOWDOWN

A Jove Book / published by arrangement with
the author

PRINTING HISTORY
Jove edition / March 1989

ISBN: 0-515-09959-7

Chapter 1

Longarm glanced again at the handcuffed man sitting beside him on the hard, unyielding, straw-upholstered seat of the Chicago & Northern day coach. His seat companion's eyes had been closed for the past half hour, but Longarm had transported too many prisoners to be deceived by appearances.

He knew that Spider Shank, the man in the seat beside him, was not only a killer, but a shrewd and merciless outlaw as well. During the time Shank had been feigning sleep, Longarm had flicked his eyes over the man regularly, and on two or three of these occasions he'd glimpsed Shank's eyeballs glinting wakefully beneath slitted lids.

"You ain't fooling me a bit, Spider," he said quietly, his voice just above a whisper.

"What do you mean, Marshal Long?" Shank asked, his eyes opening too quickly and too widely for those of a man suddenly roused from sleep.

"You don't need for me to explain what I'm talking about. All the time you acted like you were asleep I could tell you were peeking slit-eyed at me to find out if I'd dozed off or was still watching you. Now, I don't give a tinker's damn whether you're awake or asleep, and I ain't in no mind to do a lot of palavering."

1

An expression of pained surprise had formed on Shank's face while Longarm was talking. He protested, "Now, Marshal Long, you know I haven't given you no trouble since we got on this train way up at Edgemont."

"And I don't aim for you to start, either. I just want you to know that if you got any ideas about jumping through that windowpane while we're still out here in the middle of nowhere, you might as well get rid of 'em right now."

"How in hell's name do you figure I could do that? You got this handcuff so tight on my wrist that it's cutting into my arm real painful."

Longarm was so accustomed to this common complaint of his prisoners that he made no move to loosen the shackle encircling his prisoner's wrist. He said, "You got plenty of room on your half of the seat to move around and ease yourself a little bit, now that you don't have to worry about waking me up."

Glancing past Shank out the window, Longarm recognized their approximate location in the barren hillocky country of Nebraska's southwestern corner.

There was no sympathy in his voice as he said, "Anyways, we'll be pulling into Sidney in just a few minutes. I reckon you know that's where we got to change to the Union Pacific's Denver flyer, so you'll get a chance to shake away your stiffness while we're walking over to the U.P. station."

"Are we going to stop and eat a bite there?" Shank asked.

"Not likely. It's a quick change, and we'll just have time to hustle over to the U.P. depot."

"Damn it, Marshal, it's been a long time since breakfast, and you sure ain't been in no hurry to stop the butcher boy and buy a man a snack."

2

"You don't look all that starved. Besides, the government figures too close on us deputy marshals' travel allowances for me to have anything left over to buy snacks for prisoners. We'll eat our noon meal at Fred Harvey's depot restaurant in Cheyenne when the flyer makes its supper stop there."

"Well, if you're going to be hard-nosed, it looks like I'll just have to put up with it."

"That's the way it looks to me, too," Longarm said, nodding.

"I guess you know that by the time I get to the lockup in Denver, it'll be so far past suppertime that I'll have to go to bed with an empty belly!" Shank complained. "Now, that ain't fair!"

"Don't talk to me about being fair, Spider." Longarm's voice was coldly pitiless. "The time for you to think about being fair went past when you murdered a government clerk while you and your gang were robbing the mail coach. And it was a ways too late to be thinking about it when you made your getaway and killed the marshal that was taking you to the courtroom. He was a pretty good friend of mine, if you didn't know before now."

Shank opened his mouth to reply, but the look in Longarm's steel-blue eyes stopped him. Turning away, he directed his gaze out the window at the sunbaked landscape. He remained silent when the train pulled into the depot at Sidney and creaked to a halt. Longarm stood up and took out the key to his handcuffs.

"Now, I don't guess I need to tell you to behave yourself while we're changing trains," he warned his prisoner as he unlocked the shackle from the armrest of the seat and snapped it around his own wrist. "We'll be moving fast, because they don't allow no slack time."

"I guess we'll have time to go to the toilet, won't we? I got to go real bad."

"How come you didn't say so before? I'd've taken you to the men's room up in the next car."

"Because when I'm on a train I can't do a thing. All the jiggling puts me off."

"Well, I don't see the flyer on the U.P. tracks, so I guess we can take the time here," Longarm said.

He led Shank up the aisle and out of the coach. The few passengers who'd been aboard the bobtail C&N accommodation train were already starting toward the Union Pacific depot, which stood just a short distance away across the tracks. Longarm took Shank into the C&N station and stopped at the door marked MEN. He unlocked the shackle on his own wrist and stood watching as Shank stepped through the door of the cubicle.

While he waited, Longarm took out one of his long slim cigars and flicked a match into flame with his iron-hard thumbnail. He was puffing at the cheroot when he heard the tinkle of glass breaking in the men's room. One giant step took him to the door. It was locked from the inside.

Bringing up his foot, Longarm crashed his boot heel against the door. The screws that held the lock set into the doorjamb gave way with a splintering of wood. The cubicle was empty, but the broken glass shards that shone around the rim of the small high-set window in its back wall told him all that he needed to know. Swiveling, he ran with long strides to the depot door.

Blinking as his eyes adjusted to the bright sunshine, Longarm ran around to the rear of the little depot. The bobtail train that had brought him and Shank from Edgemont stood on the tracks at one side. A thin flicker of smoke rose from its stack and a man from the train

4

crew was just closing the pack box that held the oil for the pilot wheels. The small pebbles that were packed on each side of the roadbed grated under Longarm's boot heels as he ran toward the railroader.

"Did you see a fellow come outa that window yonder just a minute or so back?" Longarm called as he reached the engine.

"Can't rightly say I seen him." The man frowned and held up the big oilcan in his hand. "But while I was bending down dosing the oilbox, I heard somebody run by me."

"Could you tell which way he was heading?"

"Well, all I could tell was that he cut across the tracks in front of the hog. Sounded like he might be heading for that little string of empties yonder." Pointing toward the short string of a half-dozen boxcars that stood on a siding beyond the locomotive, the railroad man said, "He was hitting the grit pretty good, and I never did really see him, just heard him."

Longarm had already turned to look in the direction the railroader was pointing. With a nod of thanks, he ran toward the boxcars.

With one exception all the sliding side-doors of the boxcars were open. Only the door of the car that stood in the middle of the string was closed. Longarm hurried along the roadbed, glancing into each car in turn. When he reached the car with the closed door, he circled away from it. His boot heels grated loudly on the shifting rocks of the ballast as he moved, looking back frequently, but he made no effort to walk softly. When he reached the last car he looked across the tracks toward the sandy rolling humps of parched yellow soil that stretched beyond the tracks. It was a barren landscape of small undulating stone-studded baked-earth hillocks no higher than a man's thighs. Here and there clumps of olive-green sagebrush broke the monotony, but he could see no movement of their short branches. Only a moment or two of scanning the area showed him that neither the hillocks nor the scant underbrush offered more than a minimum of concealment for a fugitive.

Turning, Longarm returned to the boxcar with the closed door. Bending near a black open crack, he called, "You might as well come on out and give up, Spider. You ain't got no other choice. Was I to have to come in after you, and you jumped me, I'd have to shoot you."

For a moment there was no reply, then Spider Shank's rough voice broke the silence. "I ain't aiming to give you a chance to get rid of me all that easy, Marshal. Don't shoot! I'm coming out right now!"

Longarm pulled the boxcar door all the way open then. He stood waiting with his hands on his hips while the fugitive's feet thunked across the car's floor until he came in sight from the shadowed interior into the thin strip of sunlight that shone through the open door.

"I didn't figure I'd have much of a chance," Shank said. "But you can't blame a man for trying."

"Oh, I don't," Longarm replied. His voice was level, it held neither anger nor triumph as he went on. "I been looking for you to make a break ever since the sheriff up at Edgemont handed you over. Now let's get along fast back to the depot. That U.P. flyer don't stop here more'n a minute or two. It's due any time now, and I sure don't aim to miss it."

"Glad to see you've caught another bad one, Marshal Long," the conductor of the Union Pacific's crack train said as Longarm took out his travel vouchers and

6

handed them over. "I guess you'll want to sit with your prisoner, like always."

"I sure do, Jim," Longarm replied. "This fellow's a slick one, and he's mean as he is slippery. I aim to keep us cuffed together till I turn him over to my chief in Denver."

"We're running crowded this haul," the conductor informed him. "Just about a full load in every coach. And by the way, that includes the smoker, so you'll want to take a few quick puffs off that stogie before you toss the butt away when you get on."

Longarm nodded instead of replying. He was puffing on the long thin cigar, which was only half-consumed.

"Now, it looks like you're the last passengers," the railroader went on, "so if you don't mind waiting in the vestibule while I pass a highball up to the engineer, I'll see what I can do to accommodate you."

"I'd appreciate that," Longarm said as he nudged Spider Shank up the steps to the vestibule. "Be glad to wait."

As Longarm turned sidewise to follow Shank up the narrow steps to the vestibule, the conductor was waving his lantern to signal the engineer. By the time he'd closed and locked the vestibule door, the train was in motion, moving slowly ahead. The conductor started down the coach aisle, his head swiveling as he looked for vacant seats.

Keeping Shank in the lead, Longarm followed him. Looking ahead of the conductor he saw at a glance that except for two places, opposite each other across the aisle, the coach was full. Drawing closer to the vacant seats, Longarm could see that the seats next to them were occupied by women. The conductor had stopped and was bending over to speak to one of them. Longarm came within earshot, and over the noise of the train he could hear what the trainman was saying.

"So if you don't mind sharing the seat with that other lady across the aisle, Longarm—Marshal Long, that is —can have these seats for himself and his prisoner without taking off the man's handcuffs," the conductor was explaining. "I understand the man's dangerous and might try to escape, so that way we'll all be a lot safer."

"I don't mind a bit," the young woman occupying the seat replied. "But I do hope there's not going to be any trouble, with a criminal on board."

Longarm spoke before the conductor could reply. "I'll guarantee there won't be, ma'am. If you'll take a quick look, you can see why the conductor's asking you to move. I got to keep this handcuff on my left wrist, so I'll have my gun hand free. But mean as this fellow is, he's too smart to try anything."

"I'll rest easier, then." She smiled as she rose and stepped across the aisle. The woman in the window seat looked up, but did not speak as the passenger who was moving settled into the vacant aisle-side seat.

By now the train had picked up speed and the landscape outside seemed to be rushing past the windows. Longarm maneuvered Shank into the window seat and dropped into the aisle seat. He eased his holstered Colt into a slant that would allow a fast and easy draw and settled back, his booted feet on the rest that dropped from the bottom of the seat ahead.

As soon as he and Longarm had settled down, Spider Shank pulled his hat off and leaned back. After a moment or two of staring up at the coach ceiling, he closed his eyes and placed his hat over them, covering most of his face.

From the moment she'd made herself comfortable in

8

the seat across the aisle, the young woman who'd moved had been studying Longarm and Shank. Now she leaned toward Longarm and asked, "Is the man who's handcuffed to you really as bad as the conductor said?"

"He sure is, ma'am," Longarm answered. "He killed a U.S. Mail clerk trying to rob the mail car on a train him and his cronies were holding up. Then he got hold of a gun somehow and shot one of the deputy marshals from the office I work out of that was taking him to court in Denver during his trial."

"Then you caught him, and you're taking him back so his trial can be finished?" she asked.

"Well, now. I didn't catch him," Longarm explained. "The sheriff in a little place up in Dakota Territory recognized him from the Wanted posters we sent out and took him by surprise. The sheriff wired us in the Denver office I work out of, and I went up there to bring him back so they can finish his trial."

"He certainly does sound dangerous!" she exclaimed. "I suppose he'll almost surely be found guilty."

"Not much doubt about it," Longarm said, nodding.

While they talked, he'd been studying the woman. He placed her as being in her middle thirties, and as one of those women who were on the borderline between being beautiful and merely attractive. She was a dark brunette; her black eyebrows and a midnight-hued bun of hair visible below her narrow-brimmed straw traveling hat told him that. Her nose was a bit overlong, her cheekbones high, and her chin squared and firm. Her best features were her full red lips and overlarge brown eyes, now sparkling with interest as she leaned into the aisle to question Longarm.

"I don't know that I'd enjoy the kind of work you must have to do. It must be terribly dangerous, being a

United States marshal. I am right about that, am I not? At least, that's what the conductor said you are."

"Well, ma'am, you run into trouble now and then. But most of the time you work at it just like you do anything else. I guess it's what I'm suited for, because I sure don't aim to change."

"I can understand that," she said with a nod. "After my husband died, I had to go to work, and I didn't have too much choice. I finally got a position in a wholesale apothecary supply house, and I guess I did pretty well, because when my firm decided to open a branch office in Denver, they asked me if I'd like to move there in charge of the order office. I decided a change would do me good, so I said yes, and here I am on my way there now."

"Change never did hurt anybody I know about," Longarm said. "I'm so used to being sent places I never have been before that I've gotten used to a lot of moving around."

"Well, I've resolved one thing," she said, her voice firm. "If I like Denver, I'll stay there. If I don't, I'll go somewhere else. Men do that all the time, but from what I've seen in the business world, women aren't supposed to."

"I'd imagine you'll like Denver," Longarm told her. "It's a nice town, folks are mostly friendly."

"I suppose I'll be able to say the same thing," she agreed. "But I don't enjoy thinking about having to learn my way around."

"Shucks, ma'am, Denver's an easy place to get around in. If you..." Longarm hesitated a moment, then went on. "If you won't think I'm being too forward, it'd pleasure me to take you to supper when we pull into Denver, and after we eat I can show you around a little bit and help you get acquainted with it."

"I'd take that very kindly," she said. Then she smiled, revealing perfect white teeth. "You know, it's just occurred to me that we haven't been introduced. Since we don't have any mutual friends handy, I suppose we'll have to introduce ourselves. I'm Penelope Walford. And I heard the conductor call you by two names, Long and Longarm, so I'm just a bit confused."

"Well, Miss Walford, Long's my right name, Custis Long. But folks that know me call me Longarm whenever it suits 'em to."

"Of course! The long arm of the law!" she exclaimed, then added, "I hope you won't mind me calling you that?"

"Not one bit. And we oughta be on pretty good speaking terms by the time we get to Denver. We still got quite a while to pass before the train pulls in there."

"So we won't be strangers," she said. "And I'm already feeling better about my move. It's nice to know that I'll have one friend in Denver, even before I step off the train!"

Backing out of the hansom cab that he'd waved into service at the depot, Longarm stretched his arm as far as possible while Spider Shank alighted. Darkness was just beginning to settle over the Mile High City, but lights still glowed from several of the Federal Building's upper windows.

Sure that Chief Vail had stayed in the office in response to the telegram he'd sent from Cheyenne, Longarm hustled his prisoner up the stairs and pushed through the door into the marshal's office. To his surprise, Henry, the pink-cheeked young clerk, was still at his desk, and Chief Marshal Billy Vail stood beside him, busy signing papers.

Vail looked up when Longarm entered. "I'm glad you didn't waste any time getting here from the depot," he said. "When I got your wire from Cheyenne I arranged for the Denver police to send a man to pick up Shank here at the office and hold him until the date's set for him to stand up in court again."

"Well, that was right thoughtful of you, Billy," Longarm said. As he spoke he was unlocking the handcuff shackle that circled his wrist.

"Maybe you won't think so when I tell you why," Vail went on. "There's a new case I want you to go out on right away. All the papers are on my desk. You'll be leaving early tomorrow, so I thought it'd save time for both of us if we went over them now."

Longarm saw his plans for the evening going up in smoke. He asked Vail, "How long is this palaver going to take?"

"Only a few minutes. We can't leave the office anyhow until that city policeman comes to pick up Shank."

"What about him?" Longarm asked, tilting his head toward the prisoner.

Vail turned to Henry and said, "Sit that fellow down by your desk and keep an eye on him while Long and I are talking."

"Be glad to, Marshal Vail."

"Watch him close, too," Longarm cautioned. "He's mean and tricky."

"Don't worry. I can handle him," Henry replied as he got up and moved a chair close to his desk and gestured for Shank to sit down in it.

Billy Vail had already started toward his office door, and Longarm hurried to join him. Vail sat down behind his littered desk and began pawing through the stacks of papers looking for the documents of Longarm's new case. After a moment or two he found them and passed the thick sheaf over to Longarm.

"You take a look at them and then you can start asking—" Vail broke off as a crash sounded from the outer office.

Vail and Longarm moved at the same instant. Their chairs thudded on the carpeted floor as they both leaped up and ran for the outer office. Henry lay stretched unmoving beside his desk. There was no sign of Spider Shank.

Chapter 2

"If you're going to say I made a mistake, save it for later on," Vail snapped as Longarm opened his mouth to speak. "I admit it. But right now the important thing is to recapture that killer. You're better at running than I am. Go after him."

"He ain't got much of a head start," Longarm said. "Maybe I can luck out and catch up with him."

Turning, Longarm dashed through the office door and into the hallway, heading for the stairs. He reached them and started clattering down them, taking two steps at a time. He reached the first landing, grabbed the newel post and was swinging around it when he crashed into a uniformed city policeman who was just stepping up from the last step and onto the landing. The two men fell sprawling on the hard floor.

"What in hell are you—" the man he'd bumped into began. Then he saw who he'd collided with and said, "Longarm! What the devil's happening?"

Longarm had recognized the policeman while the two men were getting disentangled after their collision. He was Sam Hetter, one of the Denver force's veterans.

"Damn prisoner got away, Sam," he replied. "He ain't had more'n a minute or two head start. I'd guess

15

he went out about the time you were coming in down below."

"If he was, I didn't see him. It's not likely I would've paid any mind to him if I had."

"Did you pass anybody on the sidewalk outside?"

Hetter shook his head. "If I did, I sure don't remember it now. All I had on my mind was getting up to your office to talk to you about that prisoner."

"Well, come on!" Longarm exclaimed. "Maybe the two of us can catch up with him."

"Sure," Hetter said. Then as the two men started clattering down the last flight of stairs, he asked, "I guess he'd be the one I was supposed to take to the holdover for the night? Bad outlaw you was bringing back from up in Dakota Territory?"

"That's him," Longarm replied. "Name's Spider Shank."

"Oh, sure! I recall him now," Hetter said. "He's the train robber that killed a mail clerk."

"Yep, he's the one we're after," Longarm said.

By this time they'd pushed through the building's entrance doors and stepped out onto the sidewalk. Dusk was hovering above Denver, but there was still enough light remaining in the cloudless sky for them to see clearly. Stopping on the sidewalk in the cool early-evening air, they looked along the street but saw no running figure. Nor were any pedestrians in sight in either direction along Arapahoe Street.

"He's turned the corner already," Hetter said. "Now all we got to do is figure out which corner he headed for."

Nodding, Longarm replied, "Your guess'd be good as mine."

"My guess is he'd be cutting a shuck for the red-light

16

district." Hetter frowned. "That'd mean he's going north toward Larimer, either up Fifteenth or Sixteenth Street."

"Makes good sense," Longarm agreed. "You go down to the corner and try Sixteenth. I'll go the other way and turn up Fifteenth. When we get to Lawrence Street you yell if you see him, I'll do the same."

They separated then, heading for the cross streets. Longarm reached the corner and peered up the wide brick-paved street. Several blocks away he could see a hackney cab rolling north, and there were pedestrians scattered along the sidewalk, but in the growing darkness the moving figures were unrecognizable. He stood staring for a moment, then turned and started back toward the entrance doors of the Federal Building.

Down at the opposite corner Longarm could see that Hetter had also started back. They met at the door and stopped. Longarm said, "I didn't spot anybody close enough to us for them to be the son of a bitch. Did you?"

Hetter shook his head. "It's too dark, Longarm. There's alleys he could've ducked into, and once he's beat us to Larimer there's a hundred places he could run to for cover."

"Let's go back up to the office, then," Longarm suggested. "We'd best let Billy know what we aim to do."

"You're pulling me in on this?" Hetter asked as they went into the building and started upstairs.

"Oh, I wouldn't say pulling," Longarm answered. "It's up to you, Sam. Have you got anything better to do?"

"I guess not. The only orders I got was to come see you about that Shank fellow anyway."

17

"Then you'd be free to go or stay, as far as I can see."

Hetter replied slowly, "Looks like I'm already mixed up in this business too deep to back off now. If you and Billy need some help, I guess it's up to me to give it to you."

Billy Vail was alone in the outer office when Longarm and Hetter entered. He saw Longarm's eyes flicking around the room, looking for Henry.

"He's down the hall, washing his face in cold water," Vail volunteered. "And I told him to go right on home, not that he'd be any help if he stayed around."

"How'd Shank manage to get close enough to hit him?" Longarm asked.

"Hell's bells, Long! That boy's a clerk, not a deputy!" Vail replied. "He's too green to be left alone with a hard case like Shank. I've already said that's my fault. But he hit the boy with that handcuff you left on him, Long, and that's your fault."

"Then we're about square," Longarm shot back. "If you hadn't been in such an all-fired hurry to get me into your private office, I'd've taken the cuffs off of him."

"Call it even, then," Vail said. "But now that we've lost him, let's forget hows and whys and all that and get busy finding Shank again. I take it you didn't catch sight of him, or you wouldn't've come back."

"Not hide nor hair," Longarm told Vail. "But Sam and me both figure that he's likely heading for the red-light district."

"Larimer Street"—Vail nodded—"that makes good sense. And the sooner we get there the better!"

Longarm could see that his appointment with Penny Walford was going to be delayed. He pushed aside his

18

disappointment as he asked Vail, "You aim to go with me and Sam?"

"You're damned right I'm going along!" Vail answered. "And the sooner we get started, the better! Right now we're only a few minutes behind him, and once he gets into the red-light district there's a hundred hidey-holes he could duck into."

When Longarm, Vail, and Hetter reached Larimer Street, they stood for a moment studying the heart of the sporting district. As far down Larimer as they could see, the red lights gleamed, broken here and there by the brighter glows that showed above and below the batwings of the saloons and the even more brilliant light that flooded from the open doors of the gambling houses.

"Well, we're in the middle of things here," Vail observed as he turned to Hetter. "If you've got any ideas about the best place to start looking, don't be bashful about telling us."

"I been thinking about that all the way up here, Billy," Hetter said thoughtfully. "Now, from what you and Longarm was saying back at your office, this fellow we're after still had handcuffs on."

"That's right," Longarm broke in. "Unless he had a key hidden someplace on him, which ain't likely, because I searched him good when I took custody of him. He's still got my cuffs dangling from his right wrist."

"Then the first thing he'd want to do is get rid of 'em," Hetter went on. "That means he'd be looking for a locksmith."

"Sure," Vail agreed. "But how many locksmiths are going to be open for business this late?"

"Why, the kind of locksmiths I've got in mind never do close down," Hetter said. "There used to be a dozen or so of them doing business out of their back doors around the clock when I was breaking in on the force here in the district."

"You know where they're operating?" Vail asked.

"Maybe not as good as I used to. But I still come down here now and then, mainly to keep my lines out," Hetter told him. "Now, if I can run into just one or two that're doing business at their old stands, I'm pretty sure I'll be able to find out about the places where others work out of."

"Then let's get started," Longarm suggested. "Sam, why don't you give me and Billy some of the addresses to look for and we'll all three spread out and do some nosying."

Hetter shook his head. "That won't work, Longarm. You and Billy'll just have to take me along. The fellows I'm going to be looking for would shut up tighter'n a clam if you or Billy began asking 'em questions, but they'll talk to me."

"Sam's right, Long," Billy Vail agreed. "They'd know they can trust him. All they know about you and me is that we're federal lawmen." He turned to Hetter and said, "Lead the way, Sam. We'll trail along after you."

With Longarm and Vail following, Hetter started walking west on Larimer. He stopped at the gap between a dressed-stone building with the traditional red light glowing from its front window and a saloon from which laughter and the tinkle of a piano were both flowing.

"Keep in back of me, but don't get too close," he told the others. Then he turned and ducked into the narrow, evil-smelling gap that lay between the two buildings.

Longarm and Vail squeezed into the gap behind Hetter, feeling their way in the darkness that grew blacker as they got further from the street. To both men it seemed that they'd gone a good distance when Longarm bumped into Hetter and Vail in turn ran into Longarm.

"Don't talk above a whisper!" Hetter warned them, speaking in a whisper himself. "The place I'm heading for is just a step or two ahead, if the man that runs it is still around."

Longarm and Vail whispered their replies, a brief word or two from each of them signifying their understanding. Then as Hetter vanished into an even narrower crack between the back of the whorehouse and a building that faced on Market Street, they followed him, scraping the walls now and then in the tiny space.

"Stop here now, and be quiet," Hetter whispered over his shoulder. Then he rapped three quick taps and three spaced-out taps.

As faint as was the noise he made, Longarm could tell that he was rapping on a door. The metallic rasping of a key being turned in a lock broke the stillness. Then a sliver of subdued light showed the outline of a door as it opened.

"Clutty?" Hetter whispered.

"Who'd you think I'd be?" a man's voice replied. There was a pause, then he went on. "Where in hell you been, Sam? You sure ain't stopped by for a while. You looking for somebody?"

"An out-of-towner," Hetter replied. His whisper was very faint, too. "He'd be trying to find a handcuff key."

"I guess he wouldn't't've been here too long ago?" the man called Clutty asked.

"Less than a half hour."

"Yep. He was here, all right. He didn't just want a

21

handcuff key, though. He wanted a gun, too."

"That figures. Did you help him?"

"Nah. Door keys I got. Handcuff keys is scarcer'n hens' teeth." Clutty hesitated a moment, then asked, "You don't tag me in the district for a snitch if I tell you something?"

"You know I won't," Hetter whispered. "And it sure won't hurt you a bit to give us a hand in catching that fellow we're after. He's on the run for something a lot worse'n escape."

"Try Snorky, then. That's where I sent him."

"Snorky's still in the same place, I guess?"

"Yep. That shed back of Mickey's hockshop."

"I know where it is," Hetter said. "Thanks, Clutty. I'll remember this."

"You always have before," Clutty replied. "But I hope I don't have to cash my marker for a long time."

Abruptly, the slim line of light vanished and again there was the grating of a key turning in a lock. Vail began backing out of the narrow passageway. Longarm and Hetter followed him. When they reached the street again they stopped.

"I guess you heard all of what we said?" Hetter asked.

"As much as we needed to," Longarm answered. "Now, how long's it going to take us to get to this shed that fellow told you about?"

"Five minutes. It's just right up the street a ways," the policeman said.

"Then let's step out," Vail urged. "Maybe we can get to that damned outlaw before he gets his hands on another gun."

Hetter set a brisk pace as they dodged in and out among the strollers on Larimer. All of them were dawdling along, men looking for one of the three attractions the streets of the neighborhood offered: a drink, a fling at their favorite form of gambling, or a girl.

Longarm and Vail followed Hetter as he crossed Sixteenth Street and turned to cross Larimer, then kept going up Sixteenth. A few paces ahead they saw bright yellow lamplight spilling from a pair of wide windows that flanked an open door. The light was strong enough to be reflected from the three golden bells above the door, the universal wordless sign of a pawnshop.

Hetter led Longarm and Vail into the alley just beyond the pawnshop. It stood away from the building that housed the pawnshop, and lamplight spilled from a window overlooking the alley as well as outlining the door.

Stopping before they reached the area brightened by the light from the window, Hetter turned and said, "Snorky's not as edgy as Clutty. Just stand a little bit back away from us out of the light and let me do the talking, like we did before."

Without waiting for a reply, Hetter stepped up to the door and rapped lightly. He waited for a moment, then knocked a bit more vigorously. This time the door opened and light from the shed outlined a man's frame. His face was shrouded in shadow, but exposed Hetter completely.

"Evening, Snorky," Hetter said. "I heard there's a fellow nosying around looking for a handcuff key."

"So what if there is?" Snorky retorted.

"If there is, I'd like to know about it," Hetter answered. "And I figured you'd be the one to ask."

"Who's looking for him, Hetter? You and your bluecoats?"

"Just me, right now," Hetter said quickly.

23

"Then who the hell are them fellows I see back of you?"

Before Hetter could reply, the faint creak of a doorknob being turned stealthily on the opposite side of the shack reached Longarm's ears.

"That's Shank trying to get away!" Longarm told Vail. He did not bother to lower his voice. "Come on, Billy!"

Even before he'd finished speaking, light from the second door flooded the littered yard on the opposite side of the shack. Longarm and Vail were already in motion when the door was fully opened to show the outline of a moving man. Their feet pounding on the hard soil, they raced toward him.

Desk-bound and unaccustomed to quick action, Vail moved more slowly than Longarm did. The figure of the man emerging from the shack grew blurred and vanished as he ducked out of the long rectangle of light that flooded the littered yard behind the pawnshop, his boot heels thunking on the hard soil.

Longarm had targeted the fugitive's direction. His long legs churning, he raced across the yard. The man who'd come out was pounding ahead over the open area when Longarm caught up with him. Diving, he grabbed the running man around his chest, pinning his arms to his sides. Then he turned, carrying his captive with him, to bring his face into the light that spilled from the open door.

"We got what we were looking for, Billy," Longarm called. "This is Spider Shank, all right!"

"How in hell did you catch up to me, Long?" Shank asked angrily as Longarm clamped his hands together and started toward Vail.

"You ain't as smart as you figured, Shank," Longarm

replied. "You left a trail anybody could've followed."

"Damned if I see how!" Shank growled.

"I guess it's just as well you don't," Vail broke in as Longarm reached his side.

Across the yard, they could hear the voices of Hetter and Snorky raised, arguing. The distance was too great for Longarm and Vail to make out the words, but there was no mistaking the angry stridency of their voices. Then a door slammed, cutting off the voices. A moment later the yard itself went dark as the second door thudded shut.

Out of the darkness, Hetter asked, "Did you get the man you're after, Longarm?"

"We sure did," Longarm replied. He was fumbling in the darkness with his handcuff key, trying to unlock the loose shackle that dangled from Spider Shank's wrist. He finally got the wristlet open and closed it on the sullenly silent prisoner's left arm. "Thanks to you, Sam."

"If you've got him all shackled up, we can get out of here now," Vail broke in. He turned and started for the alley. Hetter and Longarm fell in beside him, the prisoner between them. Vail said, "And we won't forget how you helped us, Sam. Any time we can return the favor—"

"Don't worry about that," Hetter interrupted. "But there's something I better ask you about this prisoner."

"Ask away," Vail invited.

"Since you sent that message to headquarters for me to come pick him up, I guess you've been figuring on keeping that fellow in the city lockup until the time for his new trial?"

"Sure. Just like we always do," Vail answered.

"There's one thing wrong with your plan, Marshal

Vail. I was coming to tell you when I ran into Long-arm," the policeman said. "I guess you know about the remodeling job the aldermen have been planning for the jail?"

"I heard about it six months ago," Vail said, "but nothing since then."

"Well, they finally started it a few days ago, and right now we've got more prisoners than we can handle, with half our cells out of use. I hate to tell you this, but we just plain don't have room for him. Not a bad one, like this fellow is."

"Hmph," Vail grunted. "That sure changes my plans." He was silent for a moment as they reached the end of the alley and turned onto Larimer Street, then he said, "Long, there's a night train down to Pueblo and Canon City on the Denver and Rio Grande. I guess the only thing we can do is take him down there tonight and put him in the state pen. He'll be going there anyhow, to wait while the judge sets a date for his trial."

When Vail stopped for breath, Longarm broke in. Thinking of his planned rendezvous with Penny Wal-ford, he protested, "Now, hold on a minute, Billy! You know I don't argue much, but I just got off the train with this fellow two hours or so ago, and I've been riding on one the last two days! Why can't we wait till tomorrow to take him to Canon City?"

"I know it makes a long day for you," Vail said, "but we haven't any place to put Shank overnight. I thought about just keeping him in the office, but if we did that you'd have to stay there with him."

"Ain't there somebody else you can get to watch him, Billy?" Longarm asked. "I was figuring on—"

"I know what's bothering you, Long," Vail broke in.

"You've got a woman waiting for you somewhere. Somebody you met on the train, I guess?"

"You guessed right, but that ain't here nor there," Longarm replied. "Damn it, Billy, there's got to be somebody you can bring in to keep an eye on this fellow!"

Vail was silent for a moment, then he said, "Well, I'll say one thing. You've had it a whole lot rougher these past couple of weeks than anyone else. Go on and keep your date. I'll find someone to watch Shank tonight."

Chapter 3

"I'm real sorry that I couldn't get here any sooner," Longarm apologized to Penny Walford as she opened the door of her room in the St. James Hotel. "But I had to take on some work that I didn't figure on."

"From what you told me about your job while we were on the train, I had an idea something unexpected might have come up to delay you," she replied.

"It sure did, but that ain't important now that I finally got free."

From the moment she'd opened the door Longarm had been staring at Penny without trying to hide his admiration. She looked like a different woman than the one he'd seen on the train. She'd changed from the severely tailored travel garb she'd worn then into an equally conservative dinner gown of light-blue taffeta. The blue of the sparkling fabric was almost white. Its cut emphasized the swelling of her breasts, as well as setting off her dark hair and eyes, the clarity of her ivory skin and the sculpted curve of her full red lips. Except for a golden bracelet she wore no jewelry.

"I guess I ought to've taken time to change clothes," Longarm went on. "Except something I wasn't looking for came up and I had to tend to it."

"Something exciting, I'm sure," Penny said. "You'll have to tell me about it while we're eating, Marshal Lo— Longarm."

"Oh, it wasn't such a much. We can talk about it while we're eating supper, if you like. I guess you're about ready, late as I am."

"I'll have to confess that I'm hungry," she answered. "But I hope you won't mind when I tell you that after I'd been waiting for a while I ordered dinner to be served here in my room."

"Well . . ." Longarm hesitated for a moment, then said, "I sorta figured you might like to eat someplace where other folks could see how pretty you are."

"That's a nice compliment," Penny said. "But I didn't put this dress on for other people."

"Now, I got to tell you, I take that as a sort of compliment, ma'am—Penny," Longarm told her.

Smiling now, she said, "Please come in, Longarm, and I'll ring the call bell. As soon as the desk clerk hears it, he'll send word to the hotel dining room to start serving us."

By now Longarm had overcome his surprise. He took off his low-crowned wide-brimmed hat and stepped into the room. A small round table draped in crisp linen stood in its center. There was a bureau along one wall, and a bed along the wall opposite. Chairs were spaced between the wall and the bed, and Longarm dropped his Stetson on one of them while Penny stopped at the bell pull just inside the door and tugged it twice. Then she turned to Longarm and gestured to the chairs.

"Do sit down and be comfortable," she invited. "And

30

I noticed this evening when we got off the train that the first thing you did was to light a cigar. If you'd like one now, the smoke won't bother me a bit."

"Now, that's thoughtful, Penny, but I'd as lief wait till after supper," Longarm told her as he sat down. "Why don't you sit down while we're waiting and tell me what you think about Denver by now."

"I don't think I've made up my mind about it yet," she answered as she pulled a chair away from the wall at an angle that would allow her to face Longarm when she sat down. "But I'm ready to like it, even though I've only gotten a glimpse of it."

"I guess I better tell you to start out, Penny. I'm afraid I ain't going to be able to show you around right away," Longarm went on. "You see, the reason I'm so late is that outlaw I was bringing back from Dakota Territory. He managed to get away, and I had to help run him down again."

"You did recapture him, I hope!"

"Oh, sure. But now I got to take him to the state pen down in Canon City. I'll be gone all day tomorrow and most of the next day."

"Don't worry about a little thing like that," Penny told him. "I'll still be here when you get back."

"Well, I should hope so!" Longarm exclaimed. "And I—"

He was interrupted by a tapping on the door. Penny got up and opened it to admit a waiter pushing a cloth-draped service cart. She stepped aside to let the man enter and turned back to Longarm.

"I think we both need supper," she said. "And then perhaps we can take a short stroll, unless you're too

31

tired. I need to stretch my legs after that long ride on the train."

"I don't suppose I'll ever be too tired to do anything a lady as pretty as you asks me to," Longarm replied. "Whatever your pleasure is, I aim to do it."

"Don't be bashful about lighting your after-dinner cigar," Penny told Longarm as the waiter finished moving the small service table out of the room and closed the door. "Right now, all I want to do is sit quietly for a little while."

"I'd enjoy setting a while myself," Longarm agreed. He moved to one of the side chairs and settled into it, took out a cigar and lighted it. Then he said, "But if you want to take a stroll around Denver, we better not wait too long. Except for the saloons and gambling houses and such, there ain't much to see here at night."

"I'm not at all interested in saloons," Penny said. "I'd rather just chat with you for a while. I'm sure that with the kind of job you have, you've done a lot of things that aren't common in the part of the country I come from."

"Now, I couldn't say as to that, Penny," he said. "I don't get back East much. Once I get on the other side of the Mississippi I get a sorta feeling that I'm off my home range."

"I'll get used to it, I'm sure," she said.

In spite of what she'd said about sitting down, Penny was still standing in front of the window, looking out over the heart of the city at the scattered lights that still glowed in the business district.

"Including the climate," she went on. "Even with this window closed I can feel how cool the night air must be outside. I'll just pull the drapes together to keep it from chilling the room."

Penny tugged at the stout cord that pulled the heavy drapes together, then gave a little cry of distress.

"What's wrong?" Longarm asked.

"This pull cord's gotten twisted and somehow I've managed to get my wrist caught in it. I can't seem to get it free. I'm afraid I'll have to ask you to help me get it untangled."

"Why, sure."

Longarm put his cigar in the ash stand that stood behind his chair and stepped to the window. He took Penny's hand and tried to raise it, but the pull cord had gotten entangled in her bracelet and would not yield to his efforts. He raised her arm to look at the tangle more closely, and as he did so Penny moved, turning toward him.

She bent to look at her arm and Longarm's hands, which were busily trying to free it. The curtain cord yielded and fell away just as her movements brought her bare shoulder brushing past Longarm's chin. He felt the velvety smoothness of her skin and the faint aroma of her perfume filled his nostrils. Bending closer, Longarm pressed his lips to her shoulder and brushed them along her fragrantly scented skin to her neck, then to her cheek, and at last their lips met.

Penny turned as they embraced and Longarm felt her lips part and the tip of her moist tongue press at his lips. He met the more intimate embrace, thrusting his tongue to entwine with hers while his hands were stroking her soft shoulders. She shrugged and twisted until the straps of her gown slid away and her bare full breasts were freed.

33

Longarm felt her hands on his chest now, groping for the buttons of his shirt. He let her do the unbuttoning while he gave his entire attention, lips and tongue and fingertips, to the silky mounds of her bulging white breasts and their pebbled cherry-blush tips. Though Penny sighed now and then and was shaken by an occasional gasping shudder when Longarm's tongue rasped softly across her firm and now swollen tips, she kept her fingers busy until the last button was freed and her fingers were touching Longarm's balbriggans.

She wasted little time freeing them, and groped for the buckle of his gun belt. The belt and holstered Colt thunked to the floor, but neither she nor Longarm paid any attention to the thud of its fall. Penny was freeing the belt of Longarm's trousers, and when she'd succeeded in unbuckling it she began on the buttons of his placket until they, too, were free.

Longarm was fully erect now, and when Penny pushed his trousers and the long johns beneath them down to his thighs, she gasped at the jutting cylinder that she'd liberated and closed her hand softly around it.

"Get your boots off quick!" she urged. "I need this inside me, not just in my hand!"

Longarm wasted no time responding to her urging. He kicked away his boots and shrugged out of his shirt while Penny released him for the few seconds she needed to push his pants and long johns down his thighs into a heap at his ankles. While Longarm kicked free from his last remaining garments, he watched Penny shedding her dress and slip.

She wore nothing underneath the slip, and somehow during the course of their extended movements and caressing of the past few moments her midnight-black hair had become loosened. It fell in a cascade over her shoulders, its ends draping down to touch the equally dark and gleaming curls of her pubic bush.

Longarm stepped up to embrace her, and Penny met him with upturned face, her lips inviting his kiss. Her tongue sought his as their lips met. She lifted her arms and rested them on his shoulders and started to lever herself up. Longarm freed one arm to reach down and position himself. His fingers encountered hers, for Penny was groping at the same time to get him placed.

"Now, the bed!" she gasped in an urgent whisper as he sank into her. "Hurry!"

Longarm was moving toward the bed even as she spoke. He held her pressed to his chest and she tightened the grip of her legs around his hips as he lunged down, still holding her, and when they fell to the bed and Longarm completed his penetration she loosed a little scream of joy. Then he began thrusting and Penny's scream became a bubbling rhythmic cry as her soft body undulated in response to his lusty driving.

"Oh, this is what I've been aching for," she whispered when Longarm halted his lunges to rest. "I've been without a man far too long, but I've certainly got one now!"

Instead of replying Longarm silenced her lips with a lingering kiss. Then he began to stroke again. Penny responded quickly, and as he continued plunging into her she started trembling and at last burst into the wriggling, gasping trembling that marked the beginning of another climax.

This time Longarm did not hold back his own climax, but drove harder and faster while Penny's shrieks of fulfillment broke the stillness of the room until he joined her, and his muscular body shuddered as he found his own peak and held his body pressed to hers

35

until the ecstatic tremblings of their climax faded and they lay quiet again without breaking the fleshly bond between them. Both Longarm and Penny were tired by now, and after a short while they were asleep.

Although Longarm was accustomed by long-formed habit to wake up at the first light of dawn, he was not prepared to be roused in the night's last stage of grey darkness by the soft caresses of Penny's agile tongue and pulsing lips. He opened his eyes and saw her, a faintly outlined form in the dim room, kneeling above him. The swaying of her generous breasts fascinated him, and after he'd lain quiescent for a few moments, enjoying her attentions, he brought one hand up and began rubbing their protruding tips with his fingers.

After he'd continued his caresses for several moments Penny began quivering, but before her response passed beyond control she released him and said in a whisper, "I thought you might have to leave early. Do you, or shall I go on?"

"I don't have to get up for a while yet," he replied. "If it's your pleasure to wake me up this way, it's a sure thing that I ain't going to stop you."

"Good," she told him. "I enjoy bringing a man to life, and especially a man like you proved you were last night."

Penny resumed her gentle attentions then, and when Longarm had responded by swelling fully she knelt to straddle him. As she sank down until he filled her completely, her head thrown back with pleasure, she began rocking her hips and said, "I know you've got to leave after a while, and I want to be sure you'll be in a hurry to get back."

"You don't need to worry about that, Penny," he as-

36

sured her. "You'll be the first one I look for when I get back."

Penny swayed in silence for several minutes, then her body began trembling and her rhythm broke. Longarm pulled her to him and reversed their positions. Then he arched his back and drove with increasing force and a faster rhythm until Penny began her bubbling laugh and writhed beneath him as her ecstasy mounted.

Daylight was shining around the edges of the drawn window shades, flooding the room with half-light, before Penny's cries of completion broke the stillness and Longarm lurched forward in his final climactic lunge. Then they lay still while the room grew steadily brighter, and Longarm rose reluctantly.

"It ain't that I want to leave," he said, "but I ain't got much choice. Now, you go back to sleep if you feel like it, and I'll just sneak away. And soon as I get this new case closed, I'll be back knocking on your door again."

In spite of his virtually sleepless night, Longarm looked as fresh as the proverbial daisy when he walked into the marshal's headquarters in the Federal Building. Hetter was sitting in Henry's chair at one end of the desk, his eyes on Spider Shank, who was curled like a hairpin on the floor in front of the desk, sound asleep.

"Guess you got stuck with the watch, Sam. I see you managed to keep him corraled," Longarm said to the policeman, nodding toward the outlaw.

"Didn't take my eyes off him for a minute," Hetter replied. "He cussed for a little while, till he got too tired to talk anymore, then he went to sleep."

Shank stirred while Longarm and Hetter were talking, and started to move, but his body remained curved on the floor. Then Longarm saw what was causing the outlaw's odd curve. His wrists were handcuffed around a leg of the desk and his ankles wore shackles that had been looped by their connecting chain to the leg at the desk's far end.

"Damn it!" Shank swore. "There oughta be a law against keepin' a man curled up this way all night! I ain't never going to get my backbone straight again!"

Before Longarm or Hetter could reply, Vail's voice broke the silence. "Don't blame anybody but yourself, Shank. You got away once, so we just made damned sure you wouldn't get a chance to do it again."

Shank muttered something unhappily under his breath, but Vail was yawning and rubbing his eyes and paid no further attention to him.

"Ain't you here a mite early, Billy?" Longarm asked.

"Damn it, I've been here all night!" the chief marshal said. "And got a lot less sleep than I needed. But come on in the office. I need to lay out the whys and wherefores of that new case I've been holding up on until you got back."

"Can't that wait till I get back from Canon City?"

"Where'd you get the idea you'd be coming back here?"

"Why—" Longarm stopped short, a frown forming on his face. Then he said, "Now, wait a minute, Billy! You're not figuring to send me right on down to Arizona Territory without giving me a chance to catch my breath!"

"You can catch your breath on the way south. It'll take you three days to get to Flagstaff, and after you get off the train there you've got another two or three days to go the rest of the way to Prescott. That's enough time for an elephant to rest, Long, and you're sure not all that big. Now, let's get this done real fast. I've got a full day ahead of me and no time to waste arguing."

Longarm had seen Vail irritated too many times before not to recognize his chief's mood. He crossed to the door of Vail's private office and followed him inside. He'd seen his boss after a sleepless night before and knew better than to argue.

Even before the chief marshal settled back into his swivel chair he picked up a fat manila envelope and handed it across the desk to Longarm.

"I fixed up your travel vouchers myself last night," Vail said. "So I'll know just about where you'll be if I have to send you a wire."

"That was real thoughtful of you, Billy," Longarm said. "But I'd still like this new case a lot better if I knew what I was likely to run up against."

"Whatever it is, I imagine you'll manage to handle it," Vail told him. "Now, after you take that fellow outside down to the pen and hand him over to the warden, you cut on along to Flagstaff. It's a pretty good sized town now, after being the Santa Fe railhead for such a long time."

"Well, it's been a while since I was there last. But I guess there's bound to be a connection that'll get me down to Prescott. I don't guess you've got any idea what sort of out-of-the-way place I might be heading for?"

"That's a right good question, Long." Vail shook his head. "But I can't give you much of an answer. This case came in on the wire from Washington. The Indian Bureau headquarters there got it from their office in Arizona Territory. They're the ones that asked for you."

"And they didn't say what they want me to do?"

"They didn't give me as much information as I'd like to have, but since it's the Indian Bureau asking for you,

39

I'd say you can be pretty sure that one of the tribes down in Arizona Territory's kicking up trouble."

"Well, now"—Longarm frowned—"they got enough Indian tribes down there to fill a bushel basket and still have a few left over. They could be Utes or Apaches or Navajos or Papagos or Hopis or Chiricahuas or maybe even the Pueblos."

"You'll find out soon enough, I suppose," Vail told him. "And don't ask me any more questions, because I've told you everything I know. The only thing I'm sure of is that they want you to get there in a hurry, but they didn't say why. Right this minute you know as much about it as I do."

"I guess I better mosey on down there, then," Longarm said. "Lucky I ain't unpacked yet."

"And it's lucky I got all your travel papers together before you got in last night. All I had to worry about this morning was getting the vouchers on the Denver and Rio Grande to Canon City. It's all in that envelope. Now, if you're through asking questions, take that prisoner in there and head for the depot."

"Sure," Longarm said. "And I guess the best I can do is say that I'll be back when my case is closed."

Chapter 4

After depositing Shank in the Canon City jail, Longarm had been dozing in his seat on the westbound train when it reached a stretch of temporary tracks. He woke with a start and a sensation of falling off balance as the day coach jerked and bounced and threatened to swerve and topple off the tracks. Instinctively, he threw out his arms to help in regaining his balance, and his flailing left hand struck the upper arm and chest of the man occupying the seat beside him.

His fellow passenger had obviously been equally surprised and had awakened with the same sense of danger, for he'd now raised his own arms and was trying to push Longarm's away. Both men were blinking their eyes as wakefulness returned to them, then the rattling, swaying coach settled down as it reached the end of the detour and returned to the smoothness of the permanent tracks.

"Sorry, stranger," Longarm apologized. "It felt for a minute like we were in trouble back there."

"It did at that," the other man agreed. "But no harm done. It's the kind of thing that'll happen on almost all of these new stretches of track."

"I guess I was asleep when you got on," Longarm went on. He was pulling one of his long thin cigars from his pocket as he spoke. He took out a match, flicked his

41

thumbnail over its head and puffed his cigar to life before going on. "I know you weren't sitting here when I dozed off."

"I got on at Winslow," his seatmate explained. "And I was sitting in the car ahead of this one. But there was a family with four or five youngsters in it, and the kids got noisy and were running up and down the aisle and playing hide-and-seek and doing a lot of yelling, so I moved back to this car to get away from being disturbed. You were asleep when I sat down by you."

"That'd account for me not knowing, then," Longarm said. He glanced out the window at the landscape slipping past. It was strange to him. He turned back to the man beside him and said, "You know, I've made this run three or four times, but it don't look the same to me. You got any idea where we are?"

"We're on a new stretch of track," the other explained. "I guess you haven't heard yet that Santa Fe's changed its plans about pushing any more trackage south toward Mexico. They're going almost due west to California with their new line instead of looping down to the border."

"Then how come I got a ticket to Prescott?"

"Oh, they'll still keep an accommodation running down there to the capital. But it'll just be a spur, not mainline."

"Well, if that ain't a pretty how-de-do!" Longarm frowned. "I was figuring that they'd have their tracks pushed halfway to Mexico by now."

"You haven't been out this way for a while, I take it."

"It's been a little spell," Longarm admitted. "I guess I ought to've found out more about things changing before I left Denver, but I didn't count on running into something like this."

For a moment Longarm's seatmate sat silent, then he

42

said, "I'd say introductions are in order, since we've still got such a long way to go." He extended his hand and added, "My name's Blough, Terry Blough."

"Mine's Long, Custis Long," Longarm replied, shaking his seatmate's extended hand. "Pleased to make your acquaintance."

"Like I said, Long, we've still got quite a ways to go yet," his seatmate went on. "And I get tired of looking out the window at pretty much of nothing. I generally count on running into a card game on the train to make a long trip interesting, but nobody's seemed inclined to start one yet. If I can stir up two or three more fellows here in the smoker to get a game going, would you like to sit in?"

An alarm bell tinkled in Longarm's mind at his seatmate's smoothly handled suggestion. Blough's words had recalled the letter that Billy Vail had shown him and his fellow marshals in the Denver office a couple of months earlier. It had been a joint letter from the Western railroads, asking that all deputy marshals traveling by train be alerted to the epidemic of cardsharks, professional gamblers who'd been fleecing passengers, especially those on long trips.

His voice blandly innocent, Longarm replied, "I wouldn't say no, if it's poker you're talking about."

"That's what I had in mind," Blough said. "There's four or five men in the car that don't seem to be doing anything but looking at the scenery, what there is of it. Suppose I go along the aisle and see if any of them would be interested."

"You do that," Longarm agreed. "And I don't figure you'll have much trouble getting three more players, so while you're rounding them up, I'll see about fixing up a table in one of the seats at the back end of the car."

"Fine," Blough said. "Because I'm tired of looking

43

at nothing but bare ground and sagebrush."

On one side of the aisle both the rear seats and those in front of them were unoccupied. Longarm flipped over the backs of the pair of unoccupied seats in the next-to-last row, and racked his brain for a way to improvise a table. While he was still trying to find a solution to the problem, Blough returned with three men following him.

Blough was carrying an unusually large suitcase. It was made of dark brown leather, with fittings of gleaming brass. The smooth leather of the suitcase glowed almost as brightly as did the fittings. He glanced at the cubicle Longarm had created and nodded with satisfaction, then lifted the suitcase and placed it across the facing seats.

"Now, that'll make about as good a table as we could hope for," he said. "And I've got a little bag up in the luggage rack that I'll fetch back and use for a seat. You men have already met me, so maybe you'd like to get acquainted with each other while I step up the aisle after it."

As Blough turned away, Longarm extended his hand to the man standing nearest him. "Name's Long," he said. "Custis Long, outa Denver."

"Lafe Jacobs," the man said, shaking Longarm's hand. "I travel out of Kansas City for Russmore and Sons, saddles and boots and leather and findings."

"Adams," the other traveler said as he put out his hand. "Bob Adams. From Memphis. Patent medicines."

"Haberdashery," the third announced. "Ed Carter. I didn't catch your business, Long."

"I guess that's because I don't have what you could call a business right now, Carter," Longarm said. "Maybe the best tag you can put on me is that I'm sort of a move-around fellow, traveling west from Denver."

"Cowhand?" Carter asked.

"Oh, I've done some ranching"—Longarm nodded—"and a few other jobs, too."

Blough returned carrying a small suitcase. He opened it, took out a deck of cards, tucked them in a coat pocket, then snapped the bag closed and upended it in the aisle as he said, "Well, gentlemen, if you're ready to sit down we can get our game started."

"Any of you got any special seat where you feel lucky?" Carter asked, looking from one to another of the four.

Longarm was the first to speak. "If nobody minds, I'll hunker down here in the aisle on Blough's suitcase. My legs are a mite long. They don't fold up too good in a train seat."

Carter nodded and told the others, "I'll slide over to the window, then."

Blough picked up the big bag to let Carter sidle to the seat he'd chosen. Wordlessly, Adams sidestepped between the seats to sit facing Carter, and Jacobs dropped into the aisle seat beside Adams. Blough replaced the bag and sat down beside Carter. Longarm moved the small bag closer to the seats and hunkered down on it.

Blough took the boxed deck of cards from his coat pocket and dropped it on the suitcase as he asked, "Anybody else have a deck they'd rather use?" One by one, the others shook their heads. Blough went on, saying, "Then I guess we'll have to use these." He took the cards out of their box and spread them faceup into an arc. "It's a clean deck, gents." Gathering the cards he shuffled them twice and fanned them out facedown, then said, "Draw for the deal. High man."

Carter, sitting at Blough's left, slid out a card, then Adams, Jacobs, Longarm, and Blough made their selections. They turned the cards they'd picked faceup at almost the same time, then spent a moment studying those drawn by the others.

"Looks like I just drew the deal," Carter commented, his finger moving to the queen of diamonds that lay in front of him.

Adams had received a seven of clubs, Jacobs a three of spades, Longarm a ten of the same suit. Blough was tapping the five of diamonds that he'd pulled from the deck.

"Sure does," he agreed. He was gathering the scattered cards as he spoke, then he pushed the untidy little heap toward Carter and added, "Dealer calls the game, too. What's your pleasure, Carter?"

"I don't guess anybody'd complain if I say five-card stud with a five-dollar ante to make it interesting," Carter replied, placing a five-dollar gold piece in the center of their improvised table.

No one objected, and all of them added their antes to Carter's. Then Carter dealt, showing neither the skill of a regular gambler nor the ineptitude of a novice as he flicked a card facedown in front of each man in turn and followed it with a second card faceup.

While Carter was dealing, Longarm pulled a cigar from his vest pocket and struck a match in his usual fashion, by flicking his thumbnail across its head. He had the stogie drawing to his satisfaction and was looking at his hole card by the time Carter finished dealing the second round.

His own second card was the six of hearts and the first card lying facedown in front of him was the four of hearts. Shifting to a more comfortable position, Longarm looked around at the first faceup cards the others had been dealt.

In front of Carter lay the seven of spades. Adams had been dealt the king of diamonds and Jacobs the four of clubs. The three of hearts had fallen to Blough, who was just finishing his own survey of the displayed pasteboards.

"King bets," Carter announced.

"Well, hell, I'll put a dollar on a king any day of the week," Adams said, placing a cartwheel beside the ante money already piled in the center of the suitcase.

"And I'll always bet my first card," Jacobs remarked.

Longarm said nothing, but slid a dollar beside the pot and looked toward Blough.

"Oh, I'll go along," Blough said casually, pushing his bet toward the pot.

"So will I," Carter agreed, advancing his bet as he spoke.

"It's worth a dollar to anybody to see the next one," Blough added.

"And here that next one comes," Carter told them, flipping the cards around to each of the players.

Longarm watched them as they fell: the spade nine to Adams, the ten of clubs to Jacobs, then his own card, the two of hearts. Blough got the five of hearts and Carter flipped the spade trey beside his own cards.

"You're still high," Carter told Adams.

"I'll check this round," Adams replied, tapping the top of the suitcase.

"Now, that's a good idea"—Jacobs nodded—"so will I."

"Me, too," Longarm said.

"Ah, hell!" Blough grunted. "Let's make it more interesting than that!" He tossed a quarter-eagle into the little accumulation, the gold piece dwarfed by the silver dollars.

Without speaking, Carter pushed a half-eagle across the leather surface and subtracted from the pot the difference between it and the sum he was required to bet.

47

Adams, then Jacobs, each added two cartwheels and a half-dollar.

"I'll stay," Longarm said. He matched Blough's quarter-eagle with one of his own.

Carter dealt another card to each of them. Adams got the queen of hearts, Jacobs the four of spades, Longarm a third heart, the queen, Blough the club ace, Carter himself the eight of hearts.

"It's your bet, Jacobs," Carter announced. "Pair of fours is high right now."

"I don't imagine it'll stay high very long," Jacobs remarked. "All I'm going to do is put in a dollar so I can get a look at the last card."

"Just to be sociable, I'll go along since it only costs a dollar," Longarm remarked, adding a dollar to the pot.

"I can't let you men get out that cheap," Blough told them as he shoved out a half-eagle. "An ace is worth that much to me right now."

"I'm betting you're running a bluff," Carter said. He pushed a stack of dollars into the pot. "And I'll go along just to smoke you out."

"I wouldn't be sure of anything right now," Adams said. "But I'll see what you've got. Now, you shorts have got to put up or fold."

Without speaking, Jacobs dropped four cartwheels on the table.

"I guess that puts it up to me again," Longarm said. "And I'm curious enough to want a look at my last card."

He added the necessary four dollars to the pot. Wordlessly, Carter dealt the final cards. None of them spoke as their eyes followed his hands around the table.

He dropped the seven of clubs in front of Adams, added the ten of hearts to Jacobs's hand, and dealt Longarm the ten of clubs. Blough got the club deuce, then Carter laid the nine of hearts beside his own line of cards.

"It's dog eat dog now," Carter announced. "And Jacobs is top dog right now with those two pairs."

"Yep, and you gave him the exact same card I needed to fill out," Longarm remarked as he flipped his cards facedown. "You men can fight it out without me."

"I'll go ten dollars a pair," Jacobs announced. He added a twenty-dollar gold piece to the pot. "If I didn't mistrust what I see in front of Blough, I might go higher."

"I'm already out," Longarm reminded them as Carter looked at him questioningly. "The cards I hold ain't enough to stay in with, and I ain't such a much when I try to bluff."

Blough said, "I'll stay for this one." He put another pair of gold coins in the pot, and then two more, saying, "I've got a hunch I might have Jacobs beat."

"That sounds too rich for what I've got," Carter said. He pulled his cards together and stacked them as Longarm had earlier.

"I sure won't last," Adams said, pulling his cards into a small neat stack in front of him.

"Well, it's you and me, then," Blough told Jacobs. He stared across the table, his face expressionless. "Are you going to call me, or raise?"

"From what I'm looking at, I ought to just call," Jacobs said. "But if you expect to see what I'm holding, it'll cost you another twenty."

"I'll see you and boost you twenty more," Blough replied challengingly. He dropped two more gold pieces into the pot.

"And fifty," Jacobs answered. He pulled a long leather purse from his pocket and took out a handful of gold pieces. The other players blinked as they saw the handful of coins and sat watching while Jacobs began fingering through them.

Blough suddenly sneezed. He sniffled and sneezed again, then put his left hand into his coat pocket and drew out an oversized handkerchief. He fumbled with it a moment then held it up to his face again while another fit of sneezing took him.

Jacobs had finally found the coins he was after. He put two twenty-dollar gold pieces and a ten-dollar piece on the table and said, "Fifty dollars to you, Blough."

Blough had started to return his handkerchief to his pocket, but he lowered his hand to let it rest on the table while he picked out several coins from the heap in front of him and pushed them into the pot, saying, "You'll need another fifty on top of what you've put in if you want to see me."

Longarm had been watching the two players closely since Blough's fit of sneezing began. His eyes shifted to Jacobs as Blough moved to return his handkerchief to his pocket. When he looked across the table again he could read Jacobs's hesitation in his face. At last the frown cleared from Jacobs's face and he began fingering through his heaped-up pile of gold pieces.

"I'm in deep enough as it is," he said. "But I'll see you and raise you twenty."

"I'll see your twenty and boost you twenty more," Blough retorted challengingly.

Longarm did a bit of quick addition. His calculation told him that there was now more than three hundred dollars in the pot.

"Here's twenty, and twenty more, then," Jacobs said.

"And I'm calling you with this bet, Jacobs." Blough nodded as he shoved his bet across the suitcase. "Let's see what your hole card is."

Jacobs turned the card faceup. It was the jack of clubs. "Tens and fours are going to be pretty hard to beat," he said to Blough.

"But I've got what it takes," Blough replied as he flipped over his own hole card. It was the four of hearts. He reached out to pull the heaped-up coins toward him.

"Hold on," Longarm said. His tone was neither threatening nor loud, but Blough turned to him angrily.

"You keep outa this!" he snapped. "You've already dropped out of it, and I took it fair and square!"

"Except for one thing," Longarm replied quietly. "I just happened to see you when you switched hole cards under that handkerchief you took outa your pocket."

"Are you saying I cheated?" Blough snarled. "Because if you are, you're a double-damned liar!"

As Blough spoke he raised his right hand and snapped it sharply downward. Longarm had been resting his own hand over his vest pocket. Now he pulled his derringer out, and before Blough could bring up the sleeve gun that had dropped into his hand from the forearm holster, Longarm triggered his derringer.

Its heavy slug slammed into Blough, sending him sprawling back into the coach seat. The bullet that spat from the little sleeve gun thunked into the aisle and buried itself harmlessly in the floor as Blough's lifeless body slumped back into the coach seat.

Cries of alarm and surprise were rising from the men seated ahead of the cardplayers. Several of them had jumped to their feet when the gunshots echoed through the coach, and two or three who'd occupied aisle seats were starting for the rear of the coach.

Longarm stood up, taking his wallet from his pocket, and as he gained his feet he flipped the wallet open to show his badge.

51

"It's all right!" he called loudly. "I'm a deputy U.S. marshal, and this crook I shot drawed on me first! Just set down, now, and leave me to do my job!"

Sight of the gleaming silver badge stopped the men who'd been starting to the rear. They did not settle down at once, but stood watching.

In the sudden silence that filled the coach, Longarm announced, "All that happened was that a cardsharp tried to shoot me when I showed up his cheating! Now, go on and settle down, like I told you!"

Mutters and grumbles came from a few of the passengers, but they obeyed. When Longarm turned back to face the men who'd been in the poker game, Carter asked, "How'd you catch on to Blough's cheating?"

"I didn't at first, not even when he was switching cards under that handkerchief he pulled out," Longarm admitted. "But when he turned up that four of hearts and I recalled that I'd been holding the same card in the hand I'd folded, I knew right off he was a sharper. So I just let him play out enough rope to hang himself."

Chapter 5

"Now, I ain't trying to tell you what to do," Longarm told the conductor. He was doing his best to be patient in getting the railroader to follow his advice. The two were standing in the baggage car after wrapping Terry Blough's lifeless form in a tarpaulin and carrying the body there. Longarm went on, saying, "But was I you, I'd just let that dead man stay right here in the baggage car until this train gets to the first stop where your railroad detectives have got an office. Then turn his body over to them and let them take care of getting him buried."

"That won't be until we get to Kingman," the conductor protested. "We can't carry a dead body all that far without reporting it to the proper authorities!"

"You're looking at the proper authority right now," Longarm pointed out. "A deputy U.S. marshal's got jurisdiction anyplace where there's not any local lawmen. You oughta know that."

"But you're the one that killed this man!"

"So I am," Longarm agreed. "In the line of duty, like the law books all say."

"Well"—the conductor frowned doubtfully—"I don't see that there's anything to do except follow your advice, Marshal Long. But I hope I don't get either of us into trouble."

"Don't worry about that," Longarm assured him. "I'll put it in my report that I shot him in self-defense, and that's all either one of us will hear about it again. Now, unless you got something else we need to talk about, I'll go on back to the smoker and set down."

When Longarm stepped off the train at Prescott midmorning had arrived. The sun was high, the sky cloudless, and the clear air of Arizona Territory's high mesa country was already warmly pleasant. Several years had passed since his first visit there, but he still remembered enough of the town's layout to make a beeline for the Territorial Capitol, where the Bureau of Indian Affairs had its offices.

He took long strides, glad to be freed from his confinement in cramped and swaying railroad coaches for the past several days. The distance from the depot to the capitol building was not great and in a very few minutes Longarm was approaching the blocky grey stone structure that squatted like a fortress in the center of the town's grassed square. Now, at the beginning of summer, the new grass was just beginning to sprout, its green shoots brighter than those which had survived and grown pale during the dry winter.

There was no reason for Longarm to ask directions when he climbed the broad steps up to the capitol's wide doors. Instead of continuing up the broad flight of stairs to the main floor he took the narrower steps that led down to the basement. The sign on the frosted glass pane at the end of the corridor, BUREAU OF INDIAN AFFAIRS, told him he'd reached his destination. He pushed through the door and went inside.

Like virtually all the federal offices Longarm had ever been in, this one followed a familiar pattern. A waist-high counter spanned the room a few steps beyond the door, and at each end doors with frosted glass top-panels opened into other offices. A young clerk sat at the paper-littered desk behind the counter. He looked up when Longarm entered.

"Yes, sir," he said. "Can I help you?"

"I'm reporting to your chief. Al Clawson's the name they gave me at my office in Denver."

"You'd be—?" the clerk asked.

"Custis Long, deputy marshal outa the Denver office. Your chief likely got a wire telling him I was on the way here."

"Of course. I recall seeing the telegram now. Just a moment, Marshal Long. I'll see if Chief Clawson's busy."

Disappearing through the door of the office behind his desk, the young man returned after a moment, leaving the door to the inner office ajar. He said, "Chief Clawson said to bring you right in. If you'll come down to this end of the counter . . ."

Longarm was halfway there before the clerk had finished speaking. He stepped into the head Indian agent's office. A husky, deeply tanned man was just rising from his desk. As he extended his hand he said, "You'd be Deputy Marshal Custis Long. Glad to see you here. I was beginning to think something had delayed you."

"Nothing but the cussedness of all railroads," Longarm replied as they shook hands. "But I guess you know about what the Union Pacific's doing, building their mainline straight on west and not down this way to Mexico."

"Yes, I know." Clawson nodded. "Everybody in Coconino County's all humped up about it."

"Can't say I blame 'em," Longarm said. "And I bet a dime to a plugged penny that whatever trouble you got me here to settle up is way down in the south of the territory."

55

"You'd win your bet," Clawson told him. "It's bothering me a great deal, and there are times, like right now, when I'd like to be able to make a quick trip south myself, but I've got to be here to take care of a senate committee that'll be arriving in the next few days. I suppose you know the trouble we're having is quite a ways south of here, just on our side of the Mexican border?"

"All I know so far is that my chief said the order to send me down here came straight out of the head Indian Bureau office in Washington, which ain't what I'd call usual. I guess the big brass back there's gotten all heated up about something."

"You can blame me for that," Clawson said. "I'd heard about you catching up with those crooked Indian agents in the Indian Nation a while back, and it struck me that you might be the man for this job, too. That's why I requested the bureau to send you here."

"Suppose you tell me what's going on, then."

"Pull up a chair and sit down, Marshal Long," Clawson offered. Longarm did so, and the Indian Bureau chief said, "I told you why I asked for you. That case you settled back in the Indian Nation saved us a lot of trouble. I'm hoping you can do the same in solving the problem we've got here."

"I gathered from what my chief said back in Denver that you got a sorta ticklish situation to take care of," Longarm said.

"And it'll take a little while to acquaint you with it. But your train just got in a few minutes ago. Wouldn't you rather rest up for a little while before we get down to that?" Clawson asked.

"Oh, I ain't all that tired. And if it's all the same to you, if I got to travel far from here, I'd as lief get started early in the morning than have to put it off."

"Whatever you say," Clawson said. He sat frowning for a moment, then explained, "It's a reservation boundary dispute, down along the Gila River, and arguments like that can get right ugly sometimes, especially when there's a hotheaded rancher or two on one side and a bunch of unhappy Indians on the other."

"So I've seen," Longarm said. "I'd guess there's water rights mixed up in it, too? There generally is."

Clawson nodded. "An argument between the Papago Indians and one of the local ranchers named Rusty Barnes. The Indians claim he's stealing their water out of the Gila River."

"I was down in the south of the territory quite some ways back," Longarm said. "It was in a little place called Mina Cobre. Would that be anywhere close to where you want me to go?"

"It's quite a bit further to the southeast," Clawson said. "The reservation you'll be heading for is right on the Mexican border and stretches north for, well, a good hundred miles, and is just about the same size east and west. One thing's sure, you won't have any trouble finding it or knowing when you get where you're heading."

"You mean all I got to do is hit the Gila River and keep moving south till I run into a bunch of Papagos?"

"That's the easiest way to put it," Clawson said, nodding. "But the country down there's being settled up real fast. Once you start along the Gila River you won't have any trouble."

"As I recall it," Longarm said, "there ain't much water in the Gila till it gets on down by the Mexican border."

"Well, the Papago land runs all the way to the border. And even a drop or two of water is enough for the people in that part of the territory to kick up a fuss about."

"So the Indians claim that this Barnes fellow's taking the water that's rightfully theirs?"

"Yes, but that's only part of it," Clawson said. "They also say that he keeps trying to push the borders of his spread southeast of the river onto their reservation land."

Longarm mulled this over for a moment, then said thoughtfully, "I don't aim to be trying to tell you your business, Clawson, but it seems to me that instead of calling on our office to send me here you oughta be sending a surveyor down to that reservation to settle things once and for all."

"It's not that simple, Long. The Gila River runs through both the reservation and land that Barnes claims belongs to him. If we sent a surveyor it'd just make settling the dispute harder. Both Barnes and the Papagos would claim they'd been cheated."

"Boundary lines oughta be easy to prove," Longarm insisted.

"Not in this case," Clawson said, shaking his head. "You see, there's a stretch of about thirty miles where the river winds like a running whipsnake. It even loops back on itself a time or two. Of course, it never has been properly surveyed, and in desert country like that water's worth a lot more than gold."

"And the river don't run dry in summer?"

"Oh, it drops to nothing during the summer, when the weather gets really hot. But years and years ago the Papagos found that if they shoveled up a whole string of low dirt dams, a row of them maybe two or three miles long, each of the dams would spill into the next one as they filled up."

"I follow you," Longarm said. "A whole bunch of little ponds along the riverbed."

"And that's where they sowed their wheat," Clawson

58

went on. "They'd get one crop a year, and that was enough to tide them over until the river started flowing again during the summer runoff. It's a hell of a way to farm, but the Papagos have lived on that one crop a year for, well, nobody can really say. Maybe a hundred, two hundred years."

"I figure I can guess the rest," Longarm told the Indian Bureau man. "I'd imagine your Papagos and this rancher fellow's already been fighting about who's going to get the riverbeds?"

Again Clawson nodded. "A few wild shots from both sides is all that I've had reports of. So far there haven't been any real battles and I don't want any. That's why I sent for you. I want to get this thing settled up before a lot of blood's been spilled, and we have to call the army in."

"That sounds like you're figuring on some real trouble down there," Longarm replied.

"It could come to that," Clawson agreed. "And we're so short of good men that the only thing I could do would be to call on the army for help. And since the army never built any forts south of the Gila or west of the Santa Cruz, it'd be weeks before I could get the help I'd need to stop any trouble that might get started."

"So you want me to stop any trouble before it even starts?"

"I guess you could put it like that. But I'd guess that all you'll need to do is make peace between the Papagos and the rancher, the one that seems to be at the bottom of our trouble."

"Well, all I can do is the best I can," Longarm said. "But if I expect to do what's needed, I better start down there right away. Now, I brought my own saddle gear, it's waiting for me to pick up at the freight office in the depot. I guess your outfit can spare me a horse?"

59

"Of course. We've always got a few extra nags on hand. Our territory's not like the Indian Nation. Back there all the tribes know just exactly where their boundaries run. Out here, it's a long way between reservations."

"And I reckon you'd have all the maps and such I'd need?"

"We've got all the maps you're likely to have any use for. I'll have my clerk get busy and fix them up for you, and the travel vouchers that you'll need, too."

"Last time I had a case here, which was some years back, I stayed at the Hassayampa House." Longarm was frowning thoughtfully as he spoke. "I guess it's still doing business?"

"Just like it always has."

"And there's a place right close to it where a man can get a decent meal, as I recall. The Silver Bell, unless it's closed out. And the saloon next door to the hotel keeps Maryland rye on the back bar," Longarm went on.

"They're all just like you remember them, Marshal Long. If you'd like to settle in, I'll have the clerk get out the reports and maps you'll need. After you've settled in at the hotel, stop back by and we'll go over them together."

"That suits me to a tee," Longarm said. "And I'll be on my way to try and smooth out your Papagos and that rancher by first light tomorrow."

For the better part of a half hour Longarm had been watching the slow crawl of the sun's bright warming rays down the western wall of the wide valley. He was still chilled, for the thin night air had carried the bite he always expected to face in the West's high desert country. Dawn had just begun to brighten the eastern sky when Longarm left Prescott, and even the sight of its brightness on the valley's distant western wall improved

Longarm's spirits as his horse moved steadily south.

Poking the toe of his boot into the horse's flank to speed up the animal's gait, Longarm studied the path ahead. It was a path that obviously had seen little use in recent years, for even the deepest ruts left by wagon wheels were eroded now, and filling up. With the shadows being dispelled it became easier to follow, and Longarm allowed himself the luxury of relaxing and lighting a fresh cigar. He sat back comfortably in the saddle as his borrowed horse picked its way through the shallow canyon cut by what had once been a broad rampaging river and was now a shallow, lazy flowing creek.

As the day wore on and the valley's walls began to converge, the land ahead tilted upward. Both the creek and the reddening setting sun showed signs of disappearing, and Longarm pulled up his tiring mount and swung out of his saddle. Shortly before darkness settled over the broken land he'd eaten a cold supper from the travel rations in his saddlebags and crawled into his blanket roll.

Back in the saddle at dawn the next morning he resumed the slow, frustrating process of trying with the help of his map to decide which of the valleys would lead him to his destination the easiest and shortest way.

In that high desert country, old streambeds and the abruptly rising faces of high cliffs far outnumbered patches of level ground. Some of the towering bluffs stretched away from him for such a distance that he was unable to tell they would be mesas, and time after time he was forced to set a new course, guided by the sun's position alone, to be sure that he kept moving in the proper southerly direction.

A few of the ancient watercourses were so little different from the newer ones that Longarm found it hard to distinguish between them, and several times found himself led by the dry bed of an old river into a canyon that ended in a sharply slanting wall of stone or the vertical face of a gigantic towering cliff where a long-ago earthquake had torn the ground apart.

"Old son," he muttered as he reined in beside a small bit of ground where three living green trees stood in an expanse of short-curled desert grass that he could cross in three long steps, "this damn country ain't fit for man or beast. If it's this same way down where them Papagos and that rancher's having trouble, they'd both be showing good sense if they quit fussing and headed someplace else."

Nevertheless, he stopped at the handkerchief-sized oasis for the night when he saw the glint of fresh water in the short fuzz of vegetation. Dismounting, he worked until almost dark in widening and deepening the tiny trickle until it formed a pool large enough to allow his thirsty, tiring horse to drink. Then he spread his bedroll, and after a few bites from his travel rations and a cigar smoked slowly in the fading light, he promptly went to sleep.

Another long day's ride took Longarm out of the hilly land and onto a sweeping expanse of level country that stretched as far as his eyes could reach. Here he made quicker progress, though the map he carried lacked any details of landmarks that would allow him to check his progress or even to make sure that he was moving in the right direction. Dust was darkening the sky to the east, but in the fading light he could see a hillocky formation, a double-humped hill in silhouette that for all the world gave the appearance of a camel's back.

Taking out his map, Longarm peered at it in the fast-fading desert daylight, then breathed a deep sigh of relief when he found the word "camelback" inscribed on the map in the careful hand-printed work of its topographer.

"Well, old son," he said into the deepening dusk, "now that you know just where in hell you are, it ain't going to be too hard to figure out how to head in the way you need to go. Another two or three days, and you oughta be just about where you're supposed to. And after that, you'll just have to be ready for whatever might happen."

Of the few well-defined trails Longarm had followed during the course of his long ride from Prescott, the one he was now following bore the marks of recent use more clearly than any he'd encountered. Though he'd spared his horse as much as he possibly could when it began to show signs of tiring, the animal was limping badly now, the result of a deceptive stretch of barren landscape that had been dotted with sinkholes covered by a thin shell of hard-baked sand.

Because of this cover, the sinkholes had given no surface evidence that they existed, and the first one was quite shallow. It had only caused his horse to break stride when its hoof broke through the crust that hid it, but stepping into it brought back the old limp and the animal had almost thrown Longarm when it encountered the second one. He saw at once after it had hobbled a few steps that it had suffered a strained tendon or bruised a key leg muscle, for it had refused to move when Longarm mounted.

For a half mile or so, Longarm had led the animal, and its sore leg had seemed to have cured itself. Then, when he'd swung into the saddle and the horse had gone a short distance, its limp had returned. An overnight rest had helped, but not enough to allow it to move normally. Then, late in the previous day, when Longarm had encountered the much-used road he was now following, the crisscrossing overlapping ruts made by wagon wheels had led him to turn into it. The wide creases left by the wheels of heavily loaded wagons were new, clean-cut, and deep. From his first sight of them Longarm had been sure that they would lead him to a settlement of some kind.

His spirits still perked up, though they did not rise quite as high as they might have. The long days of slow going and the waterless overnight stop he'd been forced to make the evening before had been exhausting, even for Longarm's tough and sturdy frame, and the increasing lameness of his horse had not made the trip any brighter.

He kept looking ahead, still almost certain that the settlement indicated by a cross-hatching on his map lay only a short distance ahead, pushing back his urge to speed his lamed and tiring horse.

Chapter 6

Actually sighting the buildings he'd been expecting to see for so many weary miles was something of an anticlimax, though to Longarm it was a welcome one. His first impulse was to push his horse ahead, but he resisted the temptation and let the weary animal keep moving at its rambling faltering gait. The road—more trail than road, in reality—showed signs of regular use by a wide variety of wagons.

In the sunbaked sandy soil there were the wide deep ruts of freight wagons, the narrower lines cut by farm wagons, and the still smaller lines made by the wheels of buggies and carriages, all of them converging and crisscrossing to form a well-beaten path. After he'd first seen the roofs of the buildings, Longarm glanced up occasionally to make sure he was not being drawn to one of the abandoned settlements that had made a good beginning only to be deserted before maturity. Such places were not uncommon in the southwestern desert.

As the details of the little blur of buildings became more clearly visible, he gave a grunt of relief, for his horse was limping badly now. Sooner than he'd hoped was possible the tiny houses ahead no longer looked like the dollhouses they'd appeared to be from a distance. They seemed to grow larger and were more clearly defined with each stumbling step of his mount.

Although he chafed at his slow progress, Longarm was soon close enough to make out details of the settlement. It was obvious to him now that most of its two or three dozen houses had been standing there for a long time. There were few that did not show the uniform greyish hue created on unpainted fresh-cut lumber in such an incredibly short time by the burning sun of the dry desert. He was also close enough now to see people moving about in the small fields that surrounded the houses. At the first field he reached where there was a man working, Longarm reined in and hailed him.

"Mind telling me the name of that little town up ahead?" he called.

Stopping his work the man leaned on his hoe as he replied, "That's Hayden's Ferry. You looking for somebody special, or just pushing through?"

"That depends," Longarm answered. He'd long ago grown accustomed to having strangers answer his questions with a question of their own. He went on, saying, "If that place is a ferry, then the Gila River must be close by."

"Just past the town," the man answered. Then he repeated, "You looking for anybody in particular, or just passing by?"

"Right now I'll settle for a blacksmith shop," Longarm told the farmer. "I sure hope there's one in that town there."

"Noticed your hoss was limping," the farmer said. "You'll find old man Hayden's got a pretty good smith at his place. Just go right on through town to the river. Can't miss the Hayden place, it's right on the river-bank."

"Thanks," Longarm replied. He waved as he toed his

horse ahead, and the lame animal began moving, more reluctantly than ever now.

As small as the little town was, that it had been there for a long time was obvious to Longarm as his horse limped down its single street. The walls of its two small stores were greyed and the boards cracked by the desert sun, and even at a distance Longarm's keen eyes could see that the outer walls on many of the houses that made up the little community had suffered similar damage.

He passed the last of the houses and started up the long gentle slope that lay between town and river. Soon he caught sight of the surface of the water throwing back the sun's brightness in slowly dancing gleams between the river's curving banks. He was still a bit more than a quarter of a mile from the river when he reached the corner of a rail fence that extended along the right-hand side of the road a short distance ahead.

One side of the fence ran roughly parallel to the road and ended at the bank of the river. It was broken by a pole gate midway between the corner of the enclosed area and the road. The side of the fence that extended at a right angle from the road ran to the riverbank, which curved to make the enclosed area a rough triangle.

Within the fenced land a large rambling house stood near the riverbank at the far tip of the enclosure, and a sizable three-wall shed rose between the pole gate and the fence corner that Longarm was approaching. Moving slowly forward he could see two large anvils on log bases standing in front of the shed, and beyond the point where the rail fence met the water's edge a plank dock that extended from the bank. A large flat-bottomed scow swayed at anchor at the end of the dock, which slanted down at a gentle angle to the water's edge.

As he passed the shed Longarm saw what its bulk

had hidden from him before: two horses grazing on the shortgrass that covered the soil within the enclosed area. They were the only signs of life he saw, though a thin thread of smoke rose from the fieldstone chimney that filled almost half the end of the house. The house was the only one in sight, and Longarm was sure that it must be the one referred to by the field hand he'd talked to. Pulling up at the gate, he raised his voice.

"Hello, the house!" he called. "You got a customer out here!"

A moment passed and his hail went unanswered, but before he could call out for the second time a man appeared at the corner of the house. He started walking toward the gate, and when he'd covered enough of the distance to make shouting unnecessary, he said, "If you're wanting to go 'cross, just lift up the gate and lead your nag on over to the dock."

"I need more'n just to get across the river," Longarm told the man as he toed the horse toward the gate. "I got a lame critter here. Something wrong with its leg."

"Well, get off and lead it in, then. I'll have to look at it close if I'm going to find out what's laming it," the man replied.

Longarm swung off his horse, lifted the gate to clear the ground and pushed it open on creaking hinges, then led the horse inside. As the man from the house approached, Longarm asked, "You'd be Mr. Hayden, I reckon?"

"You reckon right. Now let's see what's wrong with your nag. Have you got any idea why it'd be favoring that near hind leg? What I mean is, did you have to cross a rock slide, or did it slip on an outcrop or anything of that sort?"

"If you've been over that trail down here from Prescott, you know how rough it is," Longarm replied. "But I can't recall anything special happening to the horse. It just started going sore on me a ways back, and it's been limping worse all the time since then."

Hayden reached the horse and after patting its rump a time or two lifted its ailing leg and examined the up-turned hoof. He studied the hoof and shoe for a moment, running his fingertips around the point where they joined, then released the hoof and turned back to Long-arm.

"I don't blame the poor critter for limping," he said. "That shoe he's got on is broken in half. It's a wonder to me he could walk on it more than a few steps."

"Think you can fix it up some way so I can keep moving?" Longarm asked. "I still got a ways to travel."

"There's not much chance you'll be riding him any time soon. His leg and hoof need to be rested a day or two, then he'll have to be fresh shod. You're welcome to stay here tonight, though."

"It's right kind of you to offer, but I'm sorta in a hurry right now," Longarm answered. "My name's Long, Custis Long. I'm a deputy U.S. Marshal down here from the Denver office on a case, and I need to keep moving to get where I'm heading."

"If you're on official business, I can certainly see why you'd want to keep moving," Hayden replied. "But you sure won't do it on this animal. You try to push him much further, he'll go lame worse than he is now. Then you'll really be in the soup."

"How about them two horses you've got in your yard here?" Longarm asked. "Can I rent one of 'em from you, and stop on my way back to pick up the one I been riding?"

"You said you're a U.S. Marshal?"

"That's right. Outa Denver. I was sent down here because the Indian Bureau needs some help on a case."

"I don't suppose you'd object to showing me your badge or warrant or whatever credentials you carry?"

"Not a bit," Longarm replied promptly. He took his wallet out and flipped it open to display his marshal's badge. "Is that enough to prove who I am?"

"Entirely adequate," Hayden replied. "I can recognize a genuine badge quite easily, Marshal Long. I happen to be the territorial judge in this district. We don't get many visitors or travelers along this road, now that the railroad line's so close. But I'm still wondering what's brought you here, so far from Denver."

"Well, the Indian Bureau asked my chief to send me because a little while ago I helped 'em out on another case, back in the Indian Nation."

"I see," Hayden answered. "That takes care of my question. Now, I'll send my foreman over to take care of your horse, and I'll be glad to loan you one of mine. Since the Indian Bureau sent you here, I assume your case involves the Papagos or the Maricopas?"

"It's the Papagos, Judge. Them and a rancher that's trying to give 'em trouble."

"A rancher?" Hayden frowned. "They generally get along pretty well with the redskins. You're sure it's not the new people who're causing the trouble? The ones who're starting to build a town on the other side of the river?"

"I didn't even know there was anything besides open range between here and the Papago reservation," Longarm replied. "And the Indian Bureau chief at Prescott didn't say anything about a new town."

"He may not know about it," Hayden said. "It's been quite a while since he's been here."

"Well, that's no business of mine," Longarm told the judge. "All I know is that the Papagos have asked the Indian Bureau for help in this trouble they're having, and I was sent here to keep the trouble from getting worse. But maybe I better not say anything else right now. You might have to judge this case if something comes up that puts it in court."

"So I might," Hayden agreed. "I won't ask any more questions, then. I'll get my man busy right away. He'll ready one of those horses over there for you to switch your saddle to, then he'll pole you across the river. Your mount will be ready by the time you're back this way."

Safely on the south side of the river and with a fresh horse under him, Longarm waved good-bye to the boatman and started along the winding wheel-rutted trail that began at the ferry slip and roughly paralleled the river's east bank. Here the Gila ran shallow in its wide, constantly curving and recurving sandy bed, a shimmering opaque sheet of water. He'd covered a very short distance along the winding trail before it forked, and the wheel ruts of the wagons curved away from the river while the less-distinct branch followed the river's winding bank.

"Damned if it ain't a funny thing the judge didn't say a word about this new trail, old son," Longarm muttered as he reined in. "Maybe he just didn't think about it. But come to think of it, he did say something about a new town going up on this side of the river. So the smart thing to do is go have a look-see. Likely somebody there'll know about whatever this trouble is between the Papagos and the rancher."

Longarm turned his horse onto the wheel-marked branch, but he'd ridden only a short distance up the long slope it crossed before he began to regret his refusal of Hayden's invitation to stay overnight. He realized belatedly that in his haste to reach his destination he'd failed to notice how close it was to sundown, and began looking around for a suitable spot where he could spend the night.

He'd ridden another half mile, while the sun vanished and the long desert twilight set in, before he saw the first place that offered a bit of shelter from the chilling wind that usually began just before midnight. It was a rock outcrop with a deep, sandy-floored crack that would just accommodate a single sleeper.

Reining up and alighting, Longarm unsaddled the horse and tethered it before lugging his saddle and saddlebags into the cleft.

After spreading his blankets, Longarm opened his saddlebags and reached for the oilskin-wrapped packet that contained his trail rations of venison jerky and parched corn. When he did not feel it, he began searching for the familiar bundle.

He touched the boxes of shells, spare ammunition for his Colt and his Winchester, the maps he'd gotten from the Indian Bureau chief, and the box of long thin cigars that he'd refilled at the tobacco shop before leaving Denver. He also found the tightly rolled pair of long johns and the extra shirt he carried.

His groping fingers encountered his spare pair of socks and a wad of bandannas, his handcuffs and a box of matches, some old, unused, outdated warrants that he hadn't yet returned to the Denver office. However, despite his rummaging and his efforts to peer inside the saddlebags in the oncoming darkness, his searching did not reveal the oilskin-wrapped trail rations of parched corn and jerky.

"Well, old son," he mused silently, "either you got careless and didn't pack that grub back in here when you stopped last time, or you lost it someplace along the trail. Now you got to go to sleep on an empty belly. Of course, it won't be the first time and likely not the last one, either."

With a philosophic sigh, he stretched out on his blankets, lighted a before-bed cigar, and puffed it until the last glow of sunset faded from the sky. Then with his hat under his head for a pillow, he closed his eyes and in three minutes was asleep.

Hunger and the chirruping cries of locusts greeting the new dawn broke Longarm's sleep before sunrise. His stomach was still demanding attention, also crying, but silently.

"Having your belly feel like your throat's been cut is what you get for being careless, old son," he muttered as he folded his saddle blanket and put it on the back of his horse. Then as he threw on his saddle and began adjusting its straps, he said, "Crying over spilt milk never helped nobody. About all you can do is start out, and sooner or later you'll run into a place where you can get some grub."

Wasting no more time, he mounted and started along the trail again. As he rode he took out one of his long thin cigars and lighted it, hoping that it would help put a stop to the rumbles and growls of his empty stomach, but they were of little help. The soft shifting sandy soil made for slow progress, and a quarter of an hour went by before he reached the top of the long gentle rise.

Then Longarm reined in and blinked with astonishment, for only a short distance away across the flat and seemingly endless alluvial plain he saw the dull gleam

73

of glass and the glow of raw new wood rising above the flat sandy ground, as well as the dark distance-diminished figures of men moving around.

"That's bound to be the place," Longarm muttered under his breath. "And it sure looks a lot bigger than the judge let on. There's got to be a lot of people who've done a big scad of work up ahead there."

Ignoring his hunger for the moment, he slapped the reins gently on the neck of his horse and toed the animal to a faster pace while he watched the clump of buildings ahead. When he'd gotten close enough to make out details, he shook his head in surprise.

"That's the start of a real town, old son," he muttered. "Even if it don't look like such a much right now."

What Longarm saw as he drew closer was a town in its beginning days rather than a town in being. In the center of the new settlement a building three or four times as big as any of the others dominated the scene. A truncated spire rose from one end of the building, though it lacked the traditional cross that would have marked it as a church.

It was also the only building in the little settlement that had been painted. Its fresh white sides gleamed in contrast to the planked walls of the rest of the buildings, which were the duller white of fresh new lumber, though here and there he saw ones which had the mellowing tan hue that comes to boards exposed to the elements for any length of time.

There were houses and the rafters and studdings of houses to be stood widely spaced on both sides of the road, and men were busy working on several of them. Few of the structures were close to the road or to the others. After he'd studied the details, which continued to become clearer, Longarm realized that the dwellings formed a pattern of recurring squares which at some future time would define streets. He was soon close enough to rein in and hail the men at work on one of the houses beside the trail.

"I don't reckon there's a restaurant here," he called. "Or maybe a saloon with a free lunch where a man can get a bite to eat at this time of day?"

"We have no restaurants yet," one of them called back. "And there will never be saloons in Mesa."

"Mesa? That's what you've named the town here?" Longarm asked.

"What better name could we choose?" the workman countered. He put aside his hammer and walked up to the side of the trail. "If you are hungry, we have brought food with us for our midday meal. We will be glad to give you some."

"Well now, that's mighty thoughtful of you," Longarm told the man.

"Then leave your saddle and come with me."

"Now, working hard the way you men are, you'll need all the grub you got with you," Longarm replied. "But from the looks of this place you're building, there's bound to be a store up ahead where I can buy some grub."

"We have no stores in Mesa yet, only a commissary where we receive the food we need for each day. And it is written in our creed that we Saints must share with those who are hungry."

Longarm had gotten his clue when he heard the word "Saints." He said, "I take it you folks that's building this town are Mormons."

"That is the word used by those who are uninitiated,

and we Saints accept it," the man replied. "Though we would rather be called brothers."

"I know," Longarm said. "I had some dealings with your brothers a while back. I won't say they acted real brotherly, but that was a pretty long time ago. What all happened then ain't neither here nor there."

For a moment the man stood in silence, then he said, "If you will not let us share with you, go to the tabernacle and ask to be fed. You will not be turned away."

"Now, I just might take you up on that," Longarm answered. "Because I got some questions I need to ask whoever's running this place here. I take it that big white building up ahead is the place for me to go?"

"Our tabernacle, yes. Bishop Remley will see to your needs and answer your questions. Tell him that Brother Jensen sent you to him."

"That'll be just fine, and I thank you for your help," Longarm told Jensen. "Now I better get along, because the day's getting older every minute, and I reckon that you and me both have a lot to do before it's over."

Chapter 7

Toeing his horse ahead, Longarm started toward the big white building that dominated the still-unfinished structures around it. He dismounted at the door and after a momentary hesitation opened it and went inside. At first glance, the building seemed empty of both furnishings and people. Then he saw a door at the far end of the long barren room and headed for it.

When he rapped on the door, the sound brought an immediate invitation to come in. The room was furnished with only a table, two chairs, and a tall wooden cabinet. A stern-looking man in his middle years sat at the table strewn with sheafs of paper, stacks of letters and a few books.

"Bishop Remley?" Longarm asked.

"Yes. And you are—?"

"Long. Curtis Long, outa the U.S. marshal's office in Denver."

A frown had formed on the bishop's face when Longarm uttered the words "U.S. marshal." He rose from his chair, the frown now becoming an angry scowl.

"Why have you been sent here?" the bishop asked. His voice and his eyes were both cold as he looked at Longarm. "To plague us with legalities? To search our houses? To command us to move elsewhere?"

"Now, just a minute, Bishop!" Longarm protested. "I ain't aiming to bust into your affairs no way at all! Why, I didn't even know there was one of your churches any-place close to here! All I came in here for was to find out something, and maybe ask if you could spare me a bite to eat."

Although the bishop's eyes did not leave Longarm's face and his grim countenance did not relax, the anger was gone from his voice when he said, "This something you came to find out, it has nothing to do with our people?"

"Not unless there's some of 'em that own ranches along the Gila River, which I take it ain't the case."

"You think correctly," Remley replied. "There are none of our faith living outside of this new community that we are trying to establish."

"Then you ain't got a thing to worry about," Longarm went on. "Now, if you'll spare me a minute more, I'll ask you what I need to know and be on my way."

"You said you were hungry." Remley frowned. "If you leave here without eating, what will you do for food?"

"Oh, I been hungry before. It don't hurt a man all that much to miss a meal now and then."

"Perhaps not," Remley said. "But I don't choose to be the one who lets you go unfed. As a favor, Marshal Long, and to spare me the pain of knowing that I had food and failed to offer it to a fellow man who is hungry, please sit down and let me share my food with you."

"Well, when you put it that way, you make it awful hard to say no," Longarm replied. "I'll be glad to do that, Bishop."

Motioning for Longarm to sit down, the bishop produced a cloth-wrapped parcel from his desk drawer. Opening it to reveal three sandwiches, he invited Longarm with a gesture to select one. Longarm picked up one of the sandwiches and bit into it, and found that between the two slices of bread there were rashers of thickly sliced bacon.

"You asked me about the ranches along the river," Remley said. "What is it that you need to know about them?"

After he'd swallowed, Longarm said, "The Indian Bureau chief up at Prescott said there's some trouble about water rights between the ranchers and the Papagos. He mentioned a rancher named Barnes was at the bottom of it. You happen to know him?"

"I've talked to him once or twice. He is not an easy man to like, Marshal Long."

"How about you folks and the Papagos?" Longarm asked, then bit into the sandwich again.

"They're not friendly toward us, any more than they are toward the ranchers. But I've observed that they seem only to wish us to let them alone. They have caused us no trouble, but we have not intruded on their lands."

After he'd swallowed, Longarm asked, "And this Barnes fellow and the other ranchers have?"

"I don't accuse anyone of anything," Remley answered quickly. "I know too little about any dispute the Indians may have with Barnes or the other ranchers along the river."

"But the Papagos have told the Indian Bureau folks that the ranchers are trying to steal their water, and they say this Barnes fellow's the ringleader. You know anything about that?"

"Nothing beyond what's common gossip," the churchman said. "I've known almost since we arrived here that there's no love lost between the ranchers and the Indians, none at all. And I'm sure you know the Papagos are a warlike tribe."

"So I've heard." By taking bites whenever the opportunity was offered by a lull in their conversation, Longarm had finished the sandwich by now. He said, "Well, Bishop, you've been a big help, and I thank you for that sandwich and ask you to excuse me for any trouble I've put you to."

"I'm very glad we've gotten acquainted," Remley said. "I hope there isn't going to be any trouble between our people and the Papagos—or the ranchers, either. We ask nothing from either of them, just the chance to live in peace."

"There won't be, provided I can talk some sense into both of 'em," Longarm assured him. He stood up and started toward the door. "Now I got to be getting along. I've used up enough of your time, and mine, too."

Outside, Longarm paused in the bright morning sunshine long enough to light a cigar while he decided which way to move. He took his map out of his saddlebag and spread it on the horse's rump to examine it. The sinuous winding lines that marked the course of the Gila River drew his attention first and he began tracing them with his forefinger, starting at Hayden's Ferry.

When he'd pinpointed as best he could the spot where he now stood, he discovered that the riverbed began curving in a huge loop just a short distance to the northeast. The river's bed swept in a series of short bends that took it north of the point where the new settlement was being built, then one sweeping curve brought it back to the south, where it slanted eastward.

80

As depicted on the map, the river's course looked like a huge keyhole, its eastern side bordering the Papago reservation and its western side flowing past the ferry.

"Well now, old son," Longarm told himself, "you ain't wasted much time and trouble, at that. All you need to do is head east till you hit the river again, then turn south. If the country you travel over's like what it is around the ferry landing, you'll be right between the Papagos and the ranchers they're fussing with." Refolding the map, Longarm returned it to his saddlebag and swung into the saddle.

For the first few miles the high desert country was even flatter than the bottom of a pancake skillet, and Longarm made good time as he rode beside the river over a carpet of short-growing grasses. Then rock outcrops appeared, breaking through the soil here and there. A few miles further the scrubby vegetation thinned and patches of shortgrass covered the light-brown soil. Both the scrub brush and the grass grew scantier as he progressed, broken by occasional rock outcrops. Around them the low-growing brush and scrub grass sprouted, as did a few stunted mesquite trees, their trunks no bigger around than a man's arm.

Soon the ground began to slope gently upward, and after Longarm had traveled a few miles, riding a short distance from the riverbank, he noticed that the river was only inches deep here, its bottom clearly visible. As he rode on, the water level dropped steadily until it became a thin sheet, then it narrowed sharply and flowed through a channel that a man on foot could span with a single long step. The shortgrass that had covered the ground on both sides of the river was now patchy and sparse.

When Longarm came to a weir that spanned the river

he reined in with a frown to examine the thick low line of small branches and clusters of dead weeds weighted down by stones. The river was a thin sheet downstream from the barrier, mere bubbling trickles that flowed in tiny rivulets here and there from the wide shallow expanse of water backed up by the low crude dam.

"Sure as God made little green apples, that just ain't natural, old son," he said into the silent air. "Somebody had to lug them rocks and weeds out there and set 'em in a line. It had to be either the Papagos or the ranchers. Question now is, which one of 'em done it, and the only way you're going to find out is to ask around."

Squinting upstream in the bright morning light, the sun glowing yellow now as the morning approached noon, Longarm could see a second weir a quarter of a mile ahead. Frowning thoughtfully, he reined his horse along the edge of the shallow pond and looked at the water's surface. It was dotted thickly with the tips of pale green plants thrusting above the surface. He rubbed his bristly chin as he studied the greenery. Although many years had passed since Longarm had left the farm his ancestors had established in the stony war-ravaged hills of West Virginia, he recognized the tips of the plants.

"Now you can fry me for a Chinaman if them little sprigs of green that's sticking up in that pond ain't real wheat heads," he muttered. "Proves you ain't as smart as you put yourself up to be, old son."

Longarm lifted himself out of the saddle and stood balancing in his stirrups while he gazed at the next weir, now only a short distance ahead. Like that of the pool where he'd stopped he saw that its surface was also pocked with the green shoots.

"Damned if that little pool up ahead ain't got wheat

growing in it too, just like this one," he assured himself as he settled back into his saddle. "And since I been traveling long enough to be on their reservation by now, it's more'n likely the Papagos fixed up these pools. Them redskins are a right sight smarter'n I gave 'em credit for being!"

During the next half mile Longarm passed two more of the small manmade ponds, each of them like the first he'd seen and all of them pocked by the small pale green shoots of wheat just emerging from the shallow water. He stopped at each pond and examined the ground around its edges. The soil beyond the rim of silt was so stone-hard that even a horse's shod hooves would have left only the shallowest kind of prints. Even if at one time there had been footprints or hoofprints along the way, the gently lapping water had done a good job of smoothing the earth at the edges of the ponds and erasing them.

Longarm toed his mount ahead. He could see the river's glinting surface for almost a mile ahead, where it swept into a curve around the face of a tall sandstone bluff. To the point where it was lost to sight he could make out the dark lines of still more weirs. Behind each of them the water was pocked by the thin points of emerging wheat stalks.

He'd covered perhaps a third of the distance to the point where the riverbed curved when the stillness was broken by the cracks of gunfire. The high-pitched shots sounded first in a series of ragged volleys. Then the rifle fire ended and the flatter sound of pistol shots echoed in deeper toned boomings. Longarm spurred his borrowed mount ahead. He reached the towering bluff that had hidden the land beyond it. A half-dozen riders, scattered widely, were galloping along the side of the high cliff, firing random shots that brought spurts of chips from its sandstone face. He glanced along the rim of the huge, almost vertical formation, but saw no signs of movement. Then the shooting grew ragged and stopped as the horsemen's pistol cylinders were emptied and the riders began converging at the base of the cliff, beside the riverbed.

With the group's attention centered on the bluff, the men on horseback had not yet seen Longarm. He watched while they gathered into a compact group at the base of the cliff and pulled up their horses. He could count them now. There were four of them, still in the saddle, clumped close together. Now and then one or another raised an arm to gesture toward the cliff or the glinting ripples of the stream at its base.

Just as Longarm had gotten almost close enough to hail the riders one of them saw him. He pointed, and his companions swiveled in their saddles to look at him. After a moment they moved toward him in a loosely spaced bunch. Longarm reined in and waited for them to reach him.

When they were within hailing distance, one of the riders called, "You ain't on open range here, stranger. This is R-B land, and I don't cotton to nobody coming onto it without I say they can!"

Longarm said nothing until the group had gotten close enough for him to speak without having to raise his voice. He said, "I didn't see no keep-off signs or no fences, friend. Everyplace where I've been, land that ain't signed or fenced is open to anybody that wants to cross it."

"There'll be signs and fences both, soon as I get around to putting 'em up," the man who'd spoken first replied. "My name's Barnes, and I happen to own this spread."

Longarm had flicked his eyes over the man while he was speaking, and had also taken quick stock of his companions. At his first glimpse of the riders he'd taken them for run-of-the-mill ranch hands, but with the closer inspection he was now giving them his sharp eyes had flashed him a warning signal.

Without appearing to do so, Longarm concentrated his attention on the hands of the man sitting his mount beside Barnes. He was holding his reins in his left hand. The back of the hand that grasped the leathers was only lightly tanned, but his right hand, which rested idly across his thigh, was the dark brown shade of a long-used and well-weathered saddle.

"Well, Barnes," Longarm said, "if I'd seen a sign or a fence I might've rode around your property. But you see, I'm a deputy United States—"

At that point, the man Longarm was watching swept his arm back as he went for his holstered revolver. His tanned hand had closed on its butt when Longarm fired. Before the weapon was clear of its holster, Longarm's Colt barked and its slug tore into the chest of the one who'd tried to draw. The man jerked and his body sagged, then he toppled from his saddle.

Barnes and the other two cowhands were going for their weapons, but Longarm's Colt had moved to cover them before they could draw. They froze, their arms in midair.

"Just set easy, he ain't going to bother nobody again and you can't help him none," Longarm told them. His voice was calm but ice-cold. "Like I started to say, I'm a deputy United States marshal. Name is Custis Long, not that it makes no never-mind. Now, just lift your guns outa their holsters with two fingers and let 'em drop to the ground. Then we'll have a little palaver."

"I'll remember this, Long! And you'll pay for it!" Barnes threatened as he and his two remaining companions obeyed Longarm's orders.

"Maybe it'd ease things up if you remembered a few things for me right now," Longarm told the angry rancher. "Like what that dead fellow's name was and when he showed up here and where he said he came from and how you came to hire him on."

"You don't wanta know much!" Barnes exploded. "What I do on my own land is nobody's business but mine!"

"Except when an officer of the law asks you about it," Longarm answered levelly.

Barnes delayed answering for only a few seconds, and his voice was sullen when he answered, "I didn't go looking for him. He just showed up at the ranch one day. Said his name was Ed Cole and he'd been a ranch hand over in New Mexico Territory."

"Cole." Longarm frowned. "Sounds a lot like Coe, don't it?"

Barnes nodded reluctantly and admitted, "A little bit, I guess. Why? What's that got to do with anything?"

"Why, there was three or four Coe brothers all mixed up in cattle thieving and such over in New Mexico Territory," Longarm said. "One of 'em sorta dropped outa sight after the others were killed in gunfights. We still got a Wanted poster out on him, and from what I remember of it, he'd fit the description on it."

"Hell, Marshal!" Barnes snorted. "If I was to try to dig into where drifters looking for jobs come from, I wouldn't have time to run my spread!"

"I'll do my own digging on this one," Longarm said.

"I was just trying to find out how well you were acquainted with him."

"I wasn't," Barnes retorted. "He showed up one day and asked if I needed another hand. It happened that I did, so I took him on. That's all I know about him."

"How long ago was that?" Longarm asked.

"Quite a while back," Barnes replied. "I don't recall the exact time. I'd say it was something like six months ago, but if it's that all-fired important I can look in my time book."

"I might just ask you to do that, later on," Longarm said. "Now I got another question for you. How far on the other side of this river does your land reach?"

"Why, it stops at the river. Which means I get the same use of it that the redskins do."

"Their land comes down to the river on the other side?"

"That's right," Barnes agreed. "I've got as much right to the water as they do, if that's any of your business."

"It just happens to be," Longarm told him. "That's why my chief sent me here. The Papagos claim you're trying to take more'n your fair share."

"So you're on their side!" Barnes snorted. "That's one hell of a note, when a man's own government won't stand up for him against a bunch of heathen Indians!"

"Hold on!" Longarm snapped. "I ain't on nobody's side! I was sent here to see that both of you're taking your fair share of water, and that's all. In case you've forgotten it, the Papagos are government wards."

"Well, what the hell do you intend to do?" Barnes demanded. "You've already killed one of my men. Are you going to try to take my water away from me next?"

"Nobody's going to take anything that's rightfully

87

yours away from you, Barnes," Longarm replied. "If you're taking water away from the Papagos, or they're taking water away from you, I'm here to settle things up so both of you'll get what's yours."

For a moment Barnes did not reply, then he said, "I guess I can't argue too much against that, seeing as I'm the one that stands to lose the most if the damned red-skins keep taking more than their share."

"I thought you might see it that way." Longarm nod-ded, then went on thoughtfully. "I got to go talk to the Papagos now, and get their side of the story. I don't reckon you'll mind taking care of this dead man while I go on to their reservation?"

"Hell, he was one of my hands till you shot the poor devil, so I guess I'm obliged to bury him."

"I'm glad you feel that way," Longarm said. "Now, I got to get moving. I oughta be able to finish up my palaver with the Papagos today, if I can get to their village before too long. Suppose I mosey along, and you take this dead man back to wherever your ranch house is and bury him. I'll stop by and talk to you again tomorrow."

"That sounds all right," Barnes replied after a mo-ment of thoughtful silence. "But I'll put you on notice right now. If you try to give them savages a drop of water more'n they're supposed to get, we'll sure as hell lock horns!"

"All I'm aiming for is to settle things fair and peace-ful," Longarm assured him.

"Well, you're talking like a sensible man now," Barnes said. "Just head to the west and a little bit south when you cross the river, and you'll get to my place in about two hours." When Longarm nodded, Barnes turned to the two men who'd been sitting silently in their saddles while he and Longarm were talking. Indicating the sprawled body on the ground, he said, "Put him across his saddle, and we'll move on."

Longarm sat watching while the cowhands completed their job. Barnes waved for them to start, then turned and nodded to Longarm and reined his horse around to follow them.

For a moment Longarm sat watching them as they moved away. Then he wheeled his horse and splashed it across the river onto the Papago reservation.

Chapter 8

While he was letting his horse pick its way across the rock-strewn bottom of the shallow Gila River, Longarm eyed the rugged country on the eastern bank. It was as different from the terrain on the other side of the river as day was from night.

Instead of the long sweep of grassed prairie he'd crossed on his way to the river, Longarm saw nothing ahead but barren hard-baked earth broken here and there by the long white reefs and humped domes of rock outcrops. A short expanse of parched and barren ground stretched beyond the area where the rocks surfaced, and past the narrow strip of level land the faces of cliffs thrust up abruptly to form a high mesa whose jagged surface-line was outlined against the pale blue sky.

"It ain't no wonder them Papagos have had to plant their wheat in the riverbed," Longarm muttered under his breath as he turned his mount onto the almost invisible trace of a trail that even his sharp eyes had almost missed seeing on the hard-baked earth. "This place ain't nothing but sand and rocks. Anybody that tried to raise a crop in country like this would just about get what the little boy shot at."

Ahead of him, the trail was barely visible on the stone-strewn hard-baked soil. Longarm flicked his eyes away from it now and then to make sure that he would not turn off into some offshoot or blind gully by mistake. Ahead and on each side of the virtually indiscernible trace he was following he got an occasional glimpse of narrow cuts and gulches that chopped up the barren land.

Now and then he glimpsed the opening of a wider than usual valley, and in some of these he could see one or two of the primitive shelters—four corner-poles and a brush-thatched roof—which he supposed housed a Papago family, though he saw no signs of any people in or near them. Ahead of him the trail wound around small mesas and jogged from one crevasse to the next.

He'd covered perhaps three or four slow miles, the trail's zigzags leading him upward most of the way, when somewhere ahead a rifle barked. Longarm saw the spurt of dust its slug kicked up from the arid soil beside the trace of a trail ahead, and his first move was one that had become an instinctive response.

Without taking his eyes off the barren gullied land that stretched in front of him, he yanked his rifle out of its saddle scabbard. Then he reined in while he studied the faint thread of powder smoke that rose in the cloudless sky a short distance ahead of him. There was no sign of movement in the area where the almost invisible wisp of smoke was dissipating rapidly, nor did another shot follow the first. Longarm lifted his rifle above his head, holding the weapon at right angles to his horse.

Raising his voice, he called, "Hold your fire, whoever you are! I ain't here to make trouble! All I want to do is palaver!"

There was no response for a moment, then a man's voice came from the broken land ahead. "Who are you? And who do you want to talk with?"

Though the speaker had only the trace of the guttural tone so common to Indians of all tribes, there was enough throatiness in it to tell Longarm that he must be a Papago.

"My name's Long, Custis Long," he called back. "I'm a deputy U.S. marshal, and the Indian Bureau in Prescott sent me here to settle whatever kind of trouble there is between you Papagos and the ranchers down along the river!"

"How do we know that you are not one of the flat-land white men who try to steal our water?" the speaker ahead asked.

"If you can see me good enough to shoot at me, I guess you can see my badge if I hold it up," Longarm suggested.

"We can see you! Hold up the badge!"

Lowering his rifle, Longarm took out his wallet and flipped it open. He held it above his head. Gleams of silver danced through the air as the badge caught the sun's rays and reflected them in the direction of the hidden Papagos. Longarm held the badge in midair for a few moments, turning it to be sure the men ahead could get a good look, then he dropped his arm.

"Well? You satisfied?" he called.

"It is enough," the Indian called back.

Stones clicked at one side of the trail ahead and Longarm turned in the direction of the sharp tapping. He saw the Indian who had risen from his hiding place beside the trail ahead walking slowly toward him. The man wore the baggy greyish white trousers and mid-thigh pullover blouse of the Papagos. Longarm looked for the rifle he'd expected the man to be carrying, but he was empty-handed.

When he'd gotten close enough for Longarm to make

out his bronzed features, Longarm saw that the man had shoulder-length black hair that showed only a few threads of grey. His face was a map of years spent in the harsh desert country that made up the southern half of Arizona Territory. Its skin was seamed and deeply wrinkled, its bronze hue darkened still further by the deep tan common to one who lives outdoors regardless of the broiling sun and harsh winds.

"Chief Clawson has sent you to help us?" were his first words as he came within speaking distance of Longarm. His English was almost unaccented.

"I guess you could say that," Longarm replied. "My name's Long. What's yours?"

"I am Aropi. My people called on me to lead them when I returned from the school at Carlisle." Aropi looked around, saw a wide, flat rock shelf protruding from the yellow soil a few steps away. Gesturing toward it, he said, "If you are not too tired from the saddle, we can talk more easily sitting down."

"What about the men you said were with you? The ones I reckon you left your rifle with."

"They will wait where they are. I did not wish to carry a gun when I came to greet you."

As they started toward the ledge, Longarm asked, "Was I hearing right when you said you were at the Indian school back East?"

"Yes. But I did not stay there as long as most. The other students were much younger than me. I spent only enough time to better my understanding of your language, then gave my place to one of our young men."

"Clawson said you Papago people are having trouble with the ranchers," Longarm began as they settled down on the rock shelf. "Except I don't know all the ins and outs of it yet, because he didn't know enough about it to tell me. That's what I'm looking for you to do, give me some idea of what's going on."

Nodding, his face still expressionless, Aropi said, "The trouble is water, but it is more than that. Did you ride along the river when you were coming here?"

"For a pretty good ways," Longarm said. "I saw your little stands of wheat in the shallows, or I guessed they were yours."

"Yes"—Aropi nodded—"it is the only place we have now to plant our grain." He waved at the parched sun-beaten landscape of the mesa's surface. Neither grass nor weeds grew anywhere in sight, but three or four widely spaced scrub pines showed grey-green branches. The Papago went on, saying, "You can see that we have no land here where we can plant a crop, not enough earth to till or enough water to keep the fields moist even if we had the land. That is why we must plant our wheat in the riverbed."

"I noticed what you were doing, with them little brush dams making pools. I reckon the way you got 'em dammed up, the water keeps running real slow from one pool to the next. But while I was looking at 'em I kept wondering if you got enough of a crop that way."

"There is enough wheat for our small tribe here. Or there would be, except for the rancher, the one called Barnes."

"He messes up your wheat?"

"Much worse than that!" Aropi exclaimed. Then he explained, "He waits until it is almost time for us to take off the wheat heads, then he brings his men and they break down our dams and take our crop to feed their cattle and horses."

"Now, I'd think he's got enough graze on the land he

95

owns to have all his herd would need," Longarm said, frowning.

"He does, of course," Aropi agreed. "He is trying to drive us from the home of our grandfathers so that he will have all the water for his cattle."

"And you let him get away with it?" Longarm asked.

"What else can we do? We were a warlike people once, when we fought the Yaquis and the Apaches to hold the little space we had along the river, below the mesa here. Then in the old days we fought beside them when the brownrobes and the soldiers from Mexico came to take the best land from all of our people. Then later on your bluecoats came and took more land than the Yaquis and the Apaches, and we have even less."

"And that's when you holed up on top of the mesa?"

"Where else was there to go? This is the only home we know, we want to keep it."

"I sure can't blame you for that. So what you want me to do is get this rancher down below to leave your wheat alone."

"We cannot eat grass, as horses and mules do, Marshal Long. And we have no wish to fight this man, for if we did he would get your government to send soldiers. We have seen what they did to the Apaches and the Yaquis."

"How long have you been letting this Barnes fellow get away with what he's been doing?"

"He started robbing us of our crop near the end of the spring harvest. We sent word to the chief at the Indian Bureau in Prescott that we needed help when we planted our late summer crop. And since then, we have waited."

"Suppose you tell me what you're figuring on me to do," Longarm suggested.

"Tell him he must stop robbing us!"

96

"I got a hunch that might be easier said than done, Aropi," Longarm replied. "I don't figure he'd listen to me any more'n he does to you folks. But I got another hunch that this Barnes is a lot more'n just a rancher. I ain't sure yet, because I got a little more digging to do, but if he's the crook I take him for, I'll maybe get him put behind bars for a good long spell."

"How can we help you?" Aropi asked.

"Right now there ain't much of a way," Longarm said, "but I'm just starting to dig. You give me time to turn over a few more shovelfuls, and let's see what I can bring up."

"In a week or two, we will have another crop of wheat ripe enough to harvest, then we must sow to get the next crop," Aropi said. "Will that give you enough time?"

"It might and it might not," Longarm answered slowly. "But if you don't see me nosying around for a few days, just hold on and don't do anything."

"You are going to this man's ranch?"

"Oh, I'll be stopping off there," Longarm promised. "But before I talk to Barnes I got to go to Hayden's Landing and pick up my horse that went lame on me while I was heading here. After that, I'll head back here and stop at Barnes's place on the way. But don't worry, Aropi. I'll be on hand when you get ready to harvest."

By pushing his horse, Longarm reached the ferry before dark the following day. The ferryboat swung gently at its mooring on the other side of the river, and there was no sign of life at Judge Hayden's place. However, there was the iron circle of an old cracked buggy tire hanging on the bottom limb of a scrub oak, and a length of strap iron dangling beside it. Longarm took the strap iron and clanged on the buggy tire until a man came running out of the barn on the Hayden property. He waved when he saw Longarm standing on the opposite bank of the river, then started for the ferryboat.

"Hope you wasn't in a hurry to get across," the ferryman said as he pushed the boat's flat prow into the short pier that served as a landing slip. "The judge rode over to Buckeye yesterday. He had to go to some kind of shindy the folks up there asked him to make a speech at, and I sorta been running behind."

"No hurry at all," Longarm answered as he led the horse down the slanting prow of the boat. "I just came by to pick up my horse, if it's over its lame spell."

"Why, it ain't quite got used to them new shoes I put on it yet," the man replied. "But the only way the critter's going to settle into 'em is to ride him a day or so. Just don't push him too hard right off. I don't imagine you'll have no trouble."

"I was sorta figuring to having a talk with the judge, too," Longarm went on. "I need to ask him a few questions."

"I ain't sure I could answer much, if it's the law you're wondering about," the man said. "But if you need to know something about this part of the territory, I might be able to help."

"Well, now," Longarm said, "I got a mite of curiosity about that rancher over by the Papago reservation. Barnes is his name."

"Anything I might be able to tell you'd be second-hand," the man said. "But the judge wouldn't likely do much better. That Barnes mostly keeps pretty much to himself. He ain't showed hair nor hide around the place here but a time or two since he taken over the old Hankens spread. Oh, he crosses now and again, but he sure don't have much to say."

"You know anything about where he comes from?"

"Someplace to the east, I've heard say," the ferryman replied. "Not the East east, like Boston or New York or Philadelphia, but he hails from Texas or Colorado or thereabouts, if I recall right."

"How big a spread has he got?"

"It ain't such a much," the ferryman said. "Hankens only taken up two sections. He always use to say he was going to file on some more, but he never got around to it."

"How many head do you figure he runs?"

"Maybe as many as two hundred, but I misdoubt it's that many. He's the same way talking about steers like Hankens was about the land, always gonna buy more, but never does."

As the boatman was finishing his remarks the ferry-boat grated on the boards of its slip. He set his pole aside, grabbed for the stout rope that ran beside the boat, and pulled it square to the landing. Longarm led his horse ashore. The ferry operator followed him after securing the boat and they started toward the barn.

"I'll go lead your nag in while you're getting your saddle ready to switch," the boatman volunteered. "If you're figuring to ride on this evening, that is."

"Well, I'd really figured on spending a little time talking to Judge Hayden," Longarm said. "But since he ain't here, I reckon I'll just push on into town. I noticed there's a saloon there when I passed through it the other day, and I suppose it's like most saloons and sets out a free lunch."

The man nodded. "Such as it is, but if you're hungry

enough to eat what they put on the table, I'd imagine you'll make out a meal."

"Anything that ain't hog swill beats parched corn and jerky out of a saddlebag," Longarm said. "Which reminds me that I got to get some of both before I start back."

"Try the general store. You'll find most everything there."

"Thanks, friend. You been real helpful. Now, if you'll tell me how much I owe you for shoeing my nag and boarding him, I'll settle up with you."

"Two dollars oughta cover it. Judge Hayden don't charge for law officers that uses the ferry."

"You're pretty sure Judge Hayden'll be back tomorrow? Because if he is, I'll just wait over for him."

"He'll be back sometime toward evening, I expect. But if you're aiming to stay the night, I ain't got no place to put you up. The judge is real persnickety about somebody sleeping in his house while he's gone."

"Would he mind if I made a shakedown in the barn?"

"He hasn't when folks has done it before. And far as I'm concerned, you're welcome to."

"I'll just ride into town, then. I got to get supper and I think I could use a drink or two."

"When you come back, just go on in the barn and make yourself comfortable, then."

"Thanks"—Longarm nodded—"it'll save me a lot of time if I can catch the judge tomorrow instead of having to make another trip back here."

Swinging up into the saddle, Longarm toed his mount ahead. He held his horse on a tight rein, giving it time to adjust to its new shoes, and night had fallen before he rode down the main and only street of the little settlement. Lights were glowing from the houses

100

that were scattered willy-nilly over the barren prairie that stretched away from both sides of the street.

Ahead there were lights spilling from the open door of the store and from the top and bottom of the saloon's batwings. Deciding that he'd better buy what he needed at the store before it closed, he reined in at the hitch rail and went inside. Behind the counter that ran the full length of the long narrow building a man stood stripping away his sleeve covers.

"Looks like you're getting ready to shut up shop," Longarm observed.

"I was," the storekeeper replied. "But it's never too late for me to wait on a customer. There ain't all that many around this place. What can I do for you this evening?"

"I need some parched corn and some jerky," Longarm said.

"That's an easy order to fill," the man told him. "About how much of each?"

"Oh, a pound or so of corn, it goes a long ways. And I generally carry two pounds of jerky, but seeing as I don't know yet how much longer I'll be traveling, I guess I better have an extra pound."

Nodding, the grocer placed a sack on the beam scale which stood on the counter, dug into an opened gunnysack that stood behind the counter, and dribbled corn into the sack until its weight balanced. He tossed the scoop back into the gunnysack. As he folded the top of the bag of corn he asked, "Just passing through, are you?"

"Not exactly," Longarm answered. "I'll likely be in the neighorhood for a while, but I doubt I'll be near enough to your town here to ride in easy if I run short on rations."

While Longarm talked the storekeeper had been sur-
veying him from boot soles to hat. Now the man asked,
"Looking for a job?"

"Oh, I already got a job. Matter of fact, that's what
brought me here."

"Business with the judge, maybe?" the storekeeper
asked, laying a slab of dark reddish brown meat on his
chopping block and reaching for the knife that was sus-
pended by a leather thong on the side of the block.
Without waiting for Longarm to reply, he asked, "You'll
want this strip-cut, I guess?"

"If it ain't too much trouble."

"No trouble at all." The grocer began taking long
thin slices off the chunk of jerky. Without looking away
from his work he said, "If you're looking for Judge
Hayden, he's gone over to Buckeye."

"So I found out," Longarm replied. "I just come
from his place. I was looking to stop and visit with
him."

"Official business?"

"I reckon you'd say it is," Longarm said. "Enough so
that I figure to stay the night and—" He broke off as a
shot sounded from the street. It was followed by a
woman's voice.

"Help!" she called. Then her feet beat a rapid tattoo
on the narrow porch in front of the store and she burst
through the door. She saw Longarm and the grocer and
said, "Help me, please! He's going to kill me if he—"
She broke off as a man's angry voice came from the
street outside.

"Libby!" he shouted. "Damn you, stop running!"

Longarm's gun hand dropped to his holster and he
swiveled toward the door as the heavier thunking of a
man's boot heels rang out. Longarm was drawing his

Colt as he turned. The woman was behind him now, cowering down.

A gun barked from the doorway as Longarm brought up the Colt. He was still in mid-turn, leveling his revolver when the flat splat of a second shot sounded behind him and the man coming through the open door reared back with the impact of the gun's slug. Then he began sagging, his revolver slipping from his hand as he sank into a heap across the threshold of the open door.

Chapter 9

For a moment or two the silence that followed the gun-shots was unbroken. Then shouts sounded from the saloon next door to the store and a half-dozen men piled out in a pushing tumble. Several of them had revolvers in their hands. Longarm took a step toward them and waved them to a halt.

"All right, now!" he said loudly. "The shooting's finished and there ain't going to be no more. Nor no more excitement, either."

"Who in hell are you?" one of them called. He and the others had stopped on Longarm's command. They stood staring at him, and those who carried revolvers in their hands made no move to holster their weapons.

"My name's Long. Deputy United States marshal."

"I guess you can show us something to prove that?" one of the men challenged.

Wordlessly, Longarm took out the wallet containing his badge and held it up for them to see.

After they'd stared in silence for a minute, one of the men asked, "Did you shoot old Tolly, Marshal?"

"No. It was the storekeeper here, and he didn't get off his shot till after the dead man had cut loose," Longarm replied levelly. "Now, I don't guess there's an undertaker in town?"

"No," one of them replied. "Nor no preacher, either. Judge Hayden always says the burying words."

"What about times like right now, when he's not around?" Longarm asked.

"Well, I hear the judge is due back tomorrow or the next day," the man who'd spoken last answered. "And I sure ain't digging no grave tonight. We'll just put off burying Tolly till the judge comes back from wherever he is."

"You can put him in my shed till then," a man in the little group volunteered. He wore a stained white apron knotted around his ample waist, the mark of a barkeep. "Then come on back in the place, and I'll set up drinks for the house. Let this lawman handle what all else has got to be done."

"He's got it tagged right," Longarm agreed. "This is my job. I'll stay here and take care of everything else."

None of the men challenged the bartender's instructions. Two of them picked up the dead man's sagging body and started toward the saloon and the others followed. Longarm turned back to face the storekeeper and the girl, who were still standing just inside the store.

"Are you going to arrest me for shooting Tolly, Marshal?" the grocer asked.

"Not so's you'd notice," Longarm assured him. "That fast shot you got off likely saved my bacon, Mr.—" He stopped, realizing that he did not know the merchant's name.

"Dawkins," the storekeeper said. "Elvis Dawkins."

"Real pleased to meet you," Longarm went on as they shook hands. "And obliged, too."

"I—I didn't see anything else that I could do," Dawkins said. He held out the little double-barreled derringer that was still in his hand and looked at it with a frown of surprise as he said, "There he was with his gun right on you, ready to shoot you. I didn't stop to think, just dropped my derringer out of my sleeve holster and shot him."

"I was wondering how you got to that gun so fast," Longarm told him. "You wear that thing all the time?"

"Just at night, when I'm keeping shop by myself. We get some pretty rough characters passing through town, Marshal. I was held up and robbed twice, then I bought this derringer and the sleeve holster for it that the gunsmith said was the best way to carry it. I've only fired it a few times, just to get the hang of it."

"I'd say you done pretty good," Longarm told Dawkins. He turned to the woman, who'd been standing staring at the open door. She was still gasping from shock and excitement, her mouth open, her eyes wide. Longarm said to her, "I'd make a guess that you and that dead man were having a real humdinger of a fuss, ma'am. And I'd make another guess that he was your husband."

"Yes," she said. "At least—well, the same thing as my husband. I guess just about everybody here in town thought Tolly and me were married, but we really weren't. We—well, we sort of got attracted to each other a little while back and set up housekeeping. But it wasn't long after that when he lost his job on the railroad they're building down south, across the desert. So we started looking and wound up here."

"That was when he found himself a new job here?" Longarm asked.

"Yes, but it hasn't been much account." She turned to the storekeeper and said, "You remember when Tolly got his job, Mr. Dawkins, helping get the streets lined up and fixed."

"Yes, I do," the merchant agreed. "But he never did show how short-tempered he was. However, that's over and done with." He turned back to Longarm and said, "Now I'd better get busy and finish fixing up your order. I imagine Miz Tolliver'd like to go home, and I expect you'll want to be moving on too."

"I—well, I want to go home all right, but I'm still sort of shaky," the young woman said to Longarm as Dawkins disappeared behind the counter.

"I can see how that'd be," Longarm told her. "I don't expect you've got far to go, though."

"No, not very," she answered. "It's just that—"

"Like you said, you're a mite shaky," Longarm said. "Now, I ain't in no hurry. Suppose you just wait here while I pick up my order. Then I'll set you in the saddle and ride crupper to your house so you won't have to go there all by yourself in the dark."

"It's not very far," she said. "And I'd really appreciate it, Marshal."

"Then just stay here," Longarm told her. "I'll be right back, and we'll have you home in no time."

Longarm went further into the store. The grocer was just folding up a paper bag into a neat bundle. He said, "Here you are, Marshal. And no charge."

"Now, I can't let you do that!" Longarm protested. "It ain't like I was paying outa my own money. I get my expenses all paid when I'm outa the office on a case."

"Then Uncle Sam won't be out of pocket." Dawkins smiled as he handed the folded bag to Longarm. "Now, I'm ready to close up, and I'm sure you've had a full day, so I'll bid you goodnight."

Longarm stepped outside and Dawkins closed the door behind him. Longarm said to the waiting woman, "Soon as I slide this little bundle into my saddlebag, I'll give you a hand up to the saddle. I hope you won't mind straddling it."

"Of course not. It's dark, and there won't be anybody around to see us."

"Soon as you're sure you're setting easy, I'll jump on the horse's rump in back of you," Longarm went on. "Then you can hand me the reins and we'll be on our way."

Longarm mounted the animal's crupper and reached around his passenger for the reins. Belatedly he remembered that he'd looped them over the saddlehorn and said, "Miz Tolliver, if you'd just loosen them reins and hand 'em back to me, I'd be mighty obliged."

"Why, of course," she replied. "I don't know much about riding on a horse." As she leaned forward and began fumbling with the leathers she said, "Could I ask a favor of you, Marshal Long?"

"Why, sure."

"Would you please call me by my first name instead of 'Mrs. Tolliver'?" She twisted in the saddle to hand Longarm the reins as she said, "I want to forget about Tolly as fast as I can. My first name is Elizabeth, but I like it better when folks just call me Libby."

"That suits me just fine," Longarm told her as he toed the horse into motion. "I got a sorta nickname I answer to, just like you have. It's Longarm. Now, which way do we wanta go?"

"Away from the ferry landing toward the edge of town. I'll tell you when to turn off the road to get to our—to my house."

Longarm's borrowed horse clopped slowly through the darkness for several minutes before Libby said, "It's just up ahead, the one behind that humped rock. I guess you've got a match handy, haven't you, Marshal Long?

I've been so upset that I can't remember exactly where I left the lamp sitting."

"Sure," he replied. "Tell you what, Libby. I'll walk you to the door and give you a match, then I'll strike one and hold it while you find the lamp and light it."

By the time they reached the house Longarm's eyes had gotten adjusted to the gloom of the moonless night. He could see the little dwelling outlined against the star-lit sky, more a cabin than a house. Reining in as close to it as possible, Longarm slid off the horse's rump and helped Libby to alight. As he walked beside her toward the cabin's shadowed walls he handed her a match and stuck another in his mouth.

Libby fumbled for a moment with the latch, then swung the door open. Longarm rasped his thumbnail across the match he'd kept handy and held it high while she went inside. Standing in the doorway, he could not make out any details of the interior until Libby lifted the chimney of a coal-oil lamp that stood on a table across the room, struck her match, and touched it to the wick. As the lamp flared into yellow light and Libby adjusted it before replacing the glass chimney, Longarm got his first real look at the interior of the little dwelling.

A partition just beyond the center point of the shanty divided it into two rooms, the one beyond the partition slightly smaller than the one in which they stood. All that Longarm could see in the rectangle of lamplight that spilled into the small room was a bed with a rumple of blankets on it. He turned his attention to the larger room

Libby was busy at the three-hole range that stood in one corner. Her back toward Longarm, she was bending down stuffing kindling splinters into its firebox. The lamp she'd lighted stood on an unpainted table in the

110

corner behind the range; two straight chairs were pulled up to the table. A narrow cot stretched from the corner behind the door, reaching almost to the dividing partition. Shelves nailed to the wall above the table held a few plates, some cups, and a heavy iron skillet and pot. A tin match safe hung from the wall near the stove. Libby straightened up and reached for a match, but Longarm moved more quickly that she did.

"Here you are," he said, flicking his thumbnail across a match head. He bent down and held the flame to a sliver of the kindling. It caught before the match had burned down, and he closed the firebox door. Then as he straightened up to face Libby he said, "Now, you just settle in for a good night's rest. Things'll look a lot better to you tomorrow."

"I suppose so," she said. "And while we were riding out here, I decided a thing or two, Longarm. Having a plan makes me feel some better already."

"I'm glad you do," Longarm told her. "But since you're safe and sound, I'll just be moseying on. I got a lot to do tomorrow, too."

"That's something else I thought about while we were getting here," Libby told him. "If you don't mind sleeping in Tolly's bed in the other room, I'd feel a lot safer if you stayed here tonight. I—I'm just not used to the idea of being alone yet."

Longarm glanced through the door of the small adjoining room, and after a moment of thoughtful silence replied, "That bed sure would be more comfortable than the ground, I bet. You're certain you won't mind me staying?"

"If I hadn't been sure, I wouldn't've asked you."

"Well, I'll just take your invitation," Longarm said.

"I ain't slept in a bed but one night since I started down here from Prescott."

"It's time you did, then," she said. "I'll go straighten out the bedclothes, then."

"While you're doing that, I'll step outside and un- saddle my horse and tether him proper and get my sad- dlebags. Why don't you just pop into bed while I take care of that? I'll blow out the lamp when I get back, and then I'll settle in, too."

"Thank you, Longarm!" Libby said. "You don't know how much better you've made me feel."

Longarm went outside and took his time handling the few chores that needed attention. When he returned to the house Libby was already in the bed in the large room, a patchwork quilt drawn up over her shoulders, her eyes shut. Longarm could not tell whether she was asleep, or had simply closed her eyes to avoid further conversation.

Moving as silently as possible, he stepped up to the table, blew out the lamp and groped his way into the small room beyond. He hung his gun belt on the corner post of the narrow bed, placing it to bring the butt of his Colt within easy grasp. Then he levered out of his boots, dropped his trousers beside them and followed them with his shirt. Then he slid between the blankets and stretched luxuriously and promptly fell asleep.

Longarm was accustomed to sleeping lightly. He woke up at once when the faint padding of bare feet on the floor near his bed reached his ears. Even in his first waking moments he was aware that Libby was the only one who could be entering the room without having dis- turbed his sleep earlier.

"Libby?" he asked. He propped himself up on an

elbow to peer in the direction from which her steps had come. In the darkness he could see her only as a white ghostly form, her chemise shrouding her from shoulders to mid-calf, her black hair invisible, but her face a white oval broken by her dark eyes and full lips. He asked, "Is there something wrong?"

"No," she replied. "Not unless I'm wrong by waking up and feeling lonesome and wanting to be close to somebody."

"You're telling me you want to crawl in bed with me?"

"Yes. That is, if you don't mind."

"You oughta know I wouldn't mind that a bit."

Longarm was moving over and lifting the blanket as he spoke. His eyes were dark-accustomed, and he watched as Libby stepped across the small space between the door and the bed. He raised a corner of the blanket and shifted as far as he could toward the wall to give her room to lie beside him. Then he draped the blanket to cover both of them. The bed was so narrow that Libby had to press close to him. The warmth of her body reached him even through his balbriggans.

"Thank you, Longarm," Libby whispered. "I guess you've had some nights when you couldn't go to sleep because you felt so lonesome. Haven't you?"

"I guess." Longarm was very aware of Libby's full breasts as she snuggled against him. He was also aware that he was in the beginning stage of an erection and shifted in the bed, trying to keep from pressing too close to Libby. He said, "I guess you were missing not having your husband around."

"Have you forgot what I told you, about Tolly not really being my husband?"

"I guess it sorta slipped my mind for a minute."

"He didn't even act like a husband," she went on. "Unless a real husband comes home drunk just about every night and piles down on his bed without saying anything to you. And acts most of the time like he'd just as soon not have you around."

"You and Tolly wasn't getting along too good?"

"Not good at all. But Tolly—well, you saw I didn't cry when Mr. Dawkins shot him."

"Come to think of it, you didn't."

"And ever since I went to bed in the other room, I've been thinking about you being in here," Libby said. "And you being by yourself and me being by myself. And I couldn't go to sleep. I kept thinking about how long it's been since somebody kissed me goodnight."

"Is that why you came in here?"

"You ought to know it is by now, Longarm," Libby replied. She shifted a bit in the bed and Longarm felt her hand on his ribs, beginning to slide down his body. Her full breasts were still pressing against him and he twisted around, trying to find enough room in the narrow bed to enable him to caress them. Libby's hand had reached Longarm's groin by now. She grasped his still incomplete erection and even through the fabric of his long johns Longarm felt the warmth of her caressing hand while she lifted her head to offer him her lips.

They clung close in a lengthy tongue-twining kiss, and though Libby had not released her grip while Longarm pulsed to a full erection, she moved her hand away now to pull up her shift. Then she turned her head to break their kiss and pressed herself full-length against Longarm, trapping his engorged shaft between their bodies.

"Hurry!" she gasped. "I don't want to wait any longer!"

114

Longarm flipped away the blanket and skinned out of his long johns while Libby pulled her night shift over her head and tossed it aside. When they touched again it was with the warm intimacy of skin against skin. Libby rotated her shoulders to rasp the budded tips of her generous breasts across the wiry curls of Longarm's chest and shuddered briefly as their bodies pressed together.

She spread her thighs then to accept him and guided his swollen shaft as he rose above her. When he felt her moist warmth ready to engulf him, Longarm thrust, a lusty lunge that buried him completely and brought a joyous murmuring sigh from her throat.

"Oh, good!" she gasped, locking her legs around his hips to hold herself to him. "Now go on, Longarm! Ride me hard and fast! You can't imagine how much I've been needing a man like you!"

Longarm responded to her by beginning to thrust in slow measured lunges that soon began to bring high-pitched sighs of pleasure from Libby's throat. As the minutes ticked past and he maintained his steady vigorous driving she started trembling and squeezing him with her legs as he neared the end of each of his downward plunges. Her sighs became small screams, and as he kept up his deep penetration while speeding the tempo of his thrusting, the small screams grew louder and closer together.

When Longarm felt her trembling in response to his driving he speeded the tempo of his lunges still more. Libby was now crying out almost constantly, silent only when she gulped air into her lungs. Her body became a turmoil of spastic shudders and at last she emptied her lungs with one great scream of total ecstasy and clung to him as her climax took her.

Longarm stopped stroking and lay with his rigid

swollen shaft buried in her willing body until her gasping subsided and her shudders faded. Then he began stroking once more. Libby was a bit slower in responding now. When her breathing once more grew ragged and her bubbling cries again began bursting from her lips he thrust with increasing speed and vigor until he felt his own spasm building.

He maintained his trip-hammer drives until Libby's climactic trembling seized her, and she could no longer control the frantic writhing heaves of her hips. Then he drove with all the vigor left in him until the bubbling half-sobs, half-joyous paeans were pouring from her lips and he relaxed the firm control he'd been maintaining and let himself slip into his own jetting climax.

For several minutes they lay motionless, then Libby broke the silence to ask, "Can we start over after we've rested a little while?"

"Why, sure," Longarm answered. "Or we can start again right now, if that's what you want to do."

"Go ahead, then," she invited. "Because I know you'll likely have to be moving on tomorrow. This is the best night I've ever spent, and I don't want it to be daylight ever again as long as you're here with me!"

Chapter 10

"Do you really have to leave today, Longarm?" Libby asked as they sat at the table finishing the breakfast she'd prepared for them.

"That'll sorta depend," he replied.

"On what?"

"On whether Judge Hayden has got back from his trip. The reason I came back here is to have a talk before I get any further along on my case."

"Then just wait for him to come back," Libby suggested. "I know a wonderful way for us to spend the time while you're waiting."

Longarm shook his head. "He might be gone a week or more, and I don't figure I can take that much time away from this case. There's real trouble in the making over on the Papago reservation, and it's my job to stop it."

"Take me with you, then."

"Now, you know I can't do that, Libby. There ain't no way I can carry you along to the places I might be going."

"I just thought I'd ask, even if I was already sure what you'd say," Libby sighed. "I guess I'll just have to settle for going on a shorter trip with you."

"Now, where'd that be?"

"Just a few steps, over to that bed," Libby replied, nodding toward the double bed that stretched along the opposite wall. "I've been looking at it ever since we sat down, asking myself why we were sitting at this table instead of being over there where we'll be a lot more comfortable and a lot closer together."

"Well, now, I never say no when a lady asks me to go someplace like that with her," Longarm replied, standing up and reaching for his belt buckle. "I'm ready if you are."

Stretched out side by side, tired but contented, they rested silently. Then Libby frowned thoughtfully and asked, "Longarm, do you know anything about that new town the Mormons are building on the other side of the river? Mesa, I hear they've named it."

"I was there a little while, but I had to move along pretty quick. Why?"

"Because I want to get away from here, and it's the closest place I know of to go."

"You don't belong to the Mormom Church, do you?"

"No. But I've got an idea that I might join it. Mormon men can have more than one wife, you know."

"So they can. Is that what you're figuring on being? Some fellow's second wife?"

"It's better than being a widow by myself," Libby retorted defiantly. "Traveling around like I did with Tolly, I saw a lot of women that didn't have husbands, and most of them—" She stopped and shook her head, then said, "Well, after what I saw, I made up my mind that there's no good place for a lone woman in country like this."

"You might be on the right track at that, Libby." Longarm nodded thoughtfully. "I tell you what. Pack up whatever you figure to take along, while I go out to Judge Hayden's and—"

"Now stop right there, Longarm!" Libby broke in.

"When I was talking about being married, I didn't mean to you!"

"It never struck my mind that you did, Libby," Longarm told her. "I've got some things to find out from the judge, but the price of a wedding license ain't one of them. In this job, it just ain't right to have a wife, because she could turn up a widow from almost any case I go out on."

"Well, it relieves my mind to hear you say that," Libby said as her frown of consternation relaxed and was replaced by a smile. "Because I've already figured out that as much as I liked last night, I couldn't endure having a husband who'd go out in the morning and leave me wondering if I'd see him walk in at suppertime or whether he'd be killed by some crook before he got back."

Longarm nodded agreement, then explained, "I got some law business to tend to with the judge about this case I'm on. He oughta be back by now from wherever he's been, but if he ain't I'll just have to set and do nothing, which is something I don't cotton to. But aside from that, whether he's back or not, he's got a horse to rent out and I'm aiming to hire it and take you up to that new town where you want to go."

"But won't that take time that you ought to spend on your case?" she asked.

"If he ain't back, all I'd be doing is waiting. Suppose you just go on and pack up while I go find out about the judge. One way or another, I aim to see you safe to where you want to go. I'll take care of my business, then we'll head on out."

Longarm saddled up and started for the ferry slip. Even before he reached the house he saw Judge Hayden's buggy standing beside it. When he got closer he could

119

see the judge himself, standing on the back porch watching his hired man tinkering with one of the buggy's wheels.

Hayden waved in greeting as Longarm reined in beside the house, and said, "If you've come to tell me you've already closed that case you're here on, Marshal Long, you're the fastest worker I've ever seen."

"Oh, I've got a while to go yet," Longarm replied as he dismounted. "Matter of fact, I've got a question or two that I need to ask you before I do much more."

"You're sure you want to talk about it with me? As I recall you were pretty closed-mouthed about it when you passed through on your way to the Papago reservation."

"That was before I knew anything about my case, Judge. But now that I've found out a little more, I ain't inclined to be so backward talking about it."

"Ask away, then," Hayden invited. "We're both working for the same boss—the folks who live in Arizona Territory."

"It's about water rights," Longarm went on.

"I had a suspicion it might be when you said you had a question," Hayden replied. "Three-quarters of the cases that the courts handle here in Arizona Territory concern water. I suppose you're talking about the Papagos and the Gila River?"

"You guess right the first time," Longarm replied.

"It's not guesswork, Long. Remember, I've lived by the Gila for a good number of years. I've got a lot of friends around hereabouts, too, and I've already heard a few whispers. There's a rancher named Barnes who's got a spread down in the Gila's big bend. I understand he's been giving the Indians trouble about the river water rights. Am I right about that being why you were sent here?"

"Right as rain, Judge."

"Then you should be on familiar ground," Hayden went on. "The law here in Arizona Territory's the same as it is just about everywhere west of the Mississippi."

"It's been a hundred years and a day since I worked on a water rights case, Judge. And I might as well lay the skinned cat on the table right now. I've only worked on two or three all the time I've been a marshal."

"I'll refresh your memory, then," the judge offered. "Water rights law is based on what lawyers and judges like me have come to call the 'arid region doctrine.' It's stood up to hundreds of court tests. What the law says is that the first person who owns land along a stream gets the rights to all the water that touches it."

"From one bank clear to the other side?"

"That's right."

"Even if somebody else buys the land on the other side?"

"Even then," the judge answered.

"That don't hardly seem right." Longarm frowned. "The last man to buy land is gonna be sucking a hind tit."

"Right or wrong, it's stood up for years, Marshal Long. If it's necessary for me to hand down a judgment, I'm bound to follow the legal precedents that've already been established."

"Knowing what's law and what ain't sure settles my mind a lot, Judge, and I thank you for telling me," Longarm said. "Now, I got to get back to work, but I'm going to need that horse I borrowed again, the one you let me use while your man was putting new shoes on mine. I hope you don't figure to be needing it for a day or so."

"You're welcome to use it, Marshal. I've got other horses. I just keep that one on the home range because it's got easy ways and anybody can handle it. Bring it back when you're through using it."

"Thanks, Judge, but I'll only need it a day or two again."

"Tell Fletch I said to saddle it up for you. Keep it as long as you need it."

"It won't be very long, a day or so. Now I better mosey along. If I have any luck, maybe I can clear this case up inside of the next few days without too much more trouble."

"I hardly know what to tell you, Marshal Long," Bishop Remley said. He looked at Libby, who was sitting beside Longarm across the table. "Or you, either, Mrs. Tolliver. Our town is far from being finished, and most of our people have barely enough room for their own families in the few small houses we've been able to build so far."

"Well, I ain't presuming to talk for Libby, here," Longarm replied. "But there's bound to be a place for her somewhere besides Hayden's Ferry."

"I don't think I could live there, after what's happened," Libby put in. "And from what I saw when we were riding into Mesa, it's going to be a nice place one of these days."

"That's our hope, too," Remley said. "And as it grows, it will become better and better."

"It can't grow without people, Bishop," Longarm reminded Remley. "That's one reason your town came to my mind as favorable when I told Libby I'd bring her here."

"Very well," Remley said. He turned to Libby and said, "I'll undertake to find some family that will take you into their home. It will probably be for a short while, but if that turns out to be the case, I'm sure there'll be another place for you. And let me be the first to welcome you as the newest resident of Mesa, Mrs. Tolliver."

Sundown was just beginning to give way to dusk by the time Longarm reached the river on his return trip from the Mormon settlement. Instead of following the trail that would have led him to Hayden's Ferry, he'd angled southwest from Mesa. The country was rough, cut by gullied canyons and small mesas, but he now had the layout of the land fixed in his mind's eye. By memory, experience, and instinct he'd reached the river at almost the exact spot he had in mind as his destination, the wide shallow stretch of water where the Papagos planted their wheat.

Turning to follow the river's course, Longarm rode at the water's edge, passing the series of pools behind the brush dams where the shoots of the Indians' wheat crop dotted the surface of the shallow placid water. His progress was slower now that the sun had left the sky. Its light-blue daytime clarity was fast giving way to the deeper blue of night by the time he reached the trail that zigzagged up the side of the mesa.

Longarm had covered only a short distance up the steep face of the towering formation before he began to debate the wisdom of continuing. The fading light was beginning to distort features of the landscape that he'd noted on his first visit to the Papagos, and even his sharp eyes were barely able now to follow the trail's upward zigzag course in the gathering gloom. His horse was breathing harder with each reluctant step, and he reined in at the first wide spot he reached on the steep winding trail.

Taking out one of his long thin cigars he lighted it and took a few satisfying puffs while his eyes stabbed the torturous slanting terrain ahead. After he'd puffed a few times, he said aloud, "Old son, if you had the brains of a constipated jackass, you'd've sure found a better place than this to stop."

While he talked, Longarm was leading his horse to a jagged rock spur that protruded from the shelving rock formation. He tied the animal there and began to spread his bedroll a few feet away from the animal. He did not try to look down into the riverbed while he worked, but resumed his soliloquy.

"Was you to try and push ahead any further all that nag'd have to do is make just one wrong step, and you'd wind up on them rocks down at the bottom squashed to a little bitty grease spot not big enough to oil up a frying pan. This place is wide enough to sleep on, so you better make do with what you got."

Puffing for a final time or two on his cigar, he dropped its butt a short distance from the inviting blankets, unstrapped his gun belt and placed it where his hand could reach the butt of his Colt in a split second. Then he squirmed between the folds of the blanket, placed his hat where it would serve him as a pillow and promptly went to sleep.

Dawn was only a reluctant hint of grey showing in the eastern sky when Longarm woke up. He lay quietly for a moment, then when no sound disturbed the chilly air of the slowly brightening day he crawled out of his blankets and levered into his boots. Stepping up to his horse, he rummaged in his saddlebags to find the packages of jerky and parched corn he'd gotten the night before and made a scanty breakfast while leaning with his back against the rough face of the stone formation to which the animal was tethered.

A swallow of water from his canteen topped off his Spartan meal, then he lighted a cigar and puffed at it while

124

he rolled his blankets and wrapped them in his poncho before strapping the neat roll behind the saddle. He was just getting ready to lift his foot to the stirrup when the soft scuffing of footsteps and the occasional sharp ticking of stone clicking against stone reached his ears.

Lifting his Winchester from its saddle scabbard, he stood waiting. The noises of someone approaching grew steadily louder, then an Indian wearing the baggy loose cotton trousers and jacket of the Papagos came into sight. Longarm returned his rifle to the scabbard and turned to greet the man.

"You'd be from Aropi's bunch, I guess," he said.

"Yes. You are the government marshal called Long?"

"That's what I answer to," Longarm replied.

"I am Nachato. Aropi sent me to meet you and bring you to him."

"How'd he know I was on the way here?"

"We have been watching the river and the land around it for many weeks, since the man Barnes began trying to take our water from us."

"You mean you could see me on the way here?"

"Of course. And on the way to the new town with the woman."

"Where's Aropi now?"

"Higher up, on top of the mesa. He did not wish to climb today. Will you come with me? We will leave your horse here, it is not far."

"Lead on, then," Longarm told the messenger. "I'll be right in back of you."

For the next quarter hour the two men moved silently as Nachato led Longarm along the narrow trail that zig-zagged upward through crevasses and across short stretches of ocher soil baked hard and worn smooth over the decades by the feet of the Papago people. It was not like the path that Longarm had taken when looking for Aropi a few days earlier. It was narrower, less well marked and a great deal steeper, and Longarm got no glimpses of the wide valleys that he'd seen before.

Several times they passed jagged yawning gaps in the broad cleft through which the trail led them before they reached the huge mesa's wind-cleft surface. In that arid land there was little difference between a footprint that had been pressed into the dry and almost sterile ground a hundred days or a hundred minutes earlier.

Aropi was waiting for them when they reached the mesa's surface. He was sitting on a flat white slab of stone that held the black marks of small fires that had been kindled on it at one time or another. He saw Longarm's puzzled frown.

"When you came here to meet me before, we stopped much lower down," he explained. "It is only when our people are in danger that we move this high on the mesa, where we can see in all directions."

"That sounds like you think there's about to be trouble," Longarm said, his frown deepening.

"Perhaps there is," the Papago responded. "I have not told you this before, Longarm, or of this place. We can see far, but not as far as Barnes's ranch, so I have sent scouts there."

"And you figure he's going to make some sort of move?"

"It may be that he will. But that is not the chief matter that troubles me."

"What is it, then?"

"Our water," Aropi replied. "This is the time when we must prepare the wheat beds for planting. Yesterday, I went with the men to help them with their work, and the first thing we saw was that the water in the river does not flow as it always did."

"Are you saying it's drying up?"

Aropi shook his head. "No, Longarm. During the years we have seen droughts, when the river fails. In a time of drought the water grows shallow slowly, but now it's level is falling quickly."

Longarm was silent for a moment, then he said, "From what you say, it sounds to me like somebody's put a dam across it."

"That is what I think, too," the Papago chief said. "Do you know how the Gila flows, Longarm?"

"Well, I studied over the map that I got at the Indian Bureau office in Prescott. But it's down below in my saddlebag. I didn't figure I'd be needing it." Longarm frowned, trying to recall the sinuous lines of the river's course that he'd seen on his map. "Seems to me I recall that it loops around a lot and makes a bunch of bends."

Aropi nodded. "The current runs north past the ferryboat crossing at Hayden's Landing and curves to the east toward the new town that your people are making. Beyond the new town it runs south in a loop around the eastern wall of this mesa, and after that it turns north at the base of the mesa, where we plant our wheat. But it turns again to the west and flows to where it goes into the river of the Yuma people."

"And that fellow Barnes who was giving you trouble rode off with his bunch to the south when they scooted away," Longarm said. "You figure it's them that's behind the river going down?"

"It could not be anyone else," Aropi replied.

"I can see that easy enough," Longarm agreed.

"One of our scouts who has been watching Barnes's ranch came back yesterday," the Papago went on. "He said that a rider from the south came there two days ago."

"Well, that ain't too much outa the way. There's men on the move around here all the time."

"Of course," Aropi agreed. "But on the next day Barnes and one of his men set off two explosions in the riverbed."

"What kind of explosions?"

"My scout did not know, but he said that water and dirt flew up and the explosion made pools in the river when it began flowing again."

"It'd have to be dynamite, then," Longarm said.

"Dynamite I have heard of, but I know nothing about it."

"Me neither," Longarm told the Papago. "But I sure can find out real fast."

"You will go there, then? To the place this man Barnes lives?"

"You're damned right I will!" Longarm exclaimed. "Just as fast as I can get down to where my horse is and fork my saddle!"

Chapter 11

"Will the white man's law allow you to take away his dynamite, if this Barnes has some?" Aropi asked.

"I ain't sure about that," Longarm answered. "But seeing as how I ain't positive, I might grab hold of it by mistake."

"But then he would only get more," the Papago said thoughtfully. "And the next time you might not be here to help us."

"I couldn't take Barnes's dynamite away from him unless I came up with a reason for arresting him too, Aropi, and he ain't on the Wanted list my department puts out regular."

"Yes, I understand that much of your white man's law," said Aropi with a nod. "I have also seen that it does not apply to those of us who do not have white skin."

"Well, between me and the Indian Bureau, we'll find a way to stop Barnes," Longarm promised. "I don't look for him to get up here and blow your folks up."

Aropi shook his head. "No. You and I agree on that. But I am sure that he does plan to explode it in the ponds where we grow our wheat. They would be useless to us if they are too deep for us to wade in while we tend our crop."

129

"Even if he did, that wouldn't get him nothing much. All you'd need to do'd be to fix 'em up again."

"It would get him nothing at once, but it would ruin our seed beds. If they were destroyed we would need years to make more in the riverbed to take the place of the ones that are there now."

"You mean it takes all that long to fix them seed beds for the wheat you grow down there?"

"I had not yet been born when we Papagos began to prepare the wheat beds, Longarm," Aropi said soberly. "My people carried good dirt from the valley and spread it on the river bottom. Much of it washed away even when the river was low, and much, much more was carried off when the current ran high with the upstream rain. Then my ancestors carried more dirt and still more, and built the shallows and learned how to put the low fences across the river. There were none of your people in our land then. A few far to the north, but none here where the desert begins."

"Well, I got to admit you got something to worry about," Longarm said soberly. "And since the Indian Bureau asked my chief to send me here, and the Indian Bureau's concerned with the fix you're in, I got to get busy and do something about that Barnes fellow."

"What will you do? Try to keep him from ruining our seed beds?"

"Oh, I'll do more than just try, Aropi," Longarm replied. "I ain't real sure exactly what I'll do, because I got some figuring to go through before I can make any sorta move."

"We will help, of course," Aropi said as a frown began forming on Longarm's face and he fell into a thoughtful silence.

Longarm did not answer, but nodded a reply. After a

few moments, he asked, "How far away is this Barnes's ranch house?"

"From the bottom of the mesa here it is a half-day's ride on a good horse that does not tire easily."

"I guess you got a good man with a horse that you can send with me to lend a hand when I go to Barnes's place?"

"More than one, if you need them. We do not have many horses, but low on the mesa we keep three or four. When do you want this man you asked about?"

"Right away, Aropi. The sooner the better. It'll take a while for us to get to Barnes's place, and I want to get there while its light enough to give us a good look-see."

"You will have him at once," the Papago chief promised. "I will send Shawahawaki with you. He is a young man, and knows your language well."

"I ain't real sure he'll need a rifle, but if he's got one I'd say he best bring it along."

Aropi nodded, then asked, "Do you think there will be shooting?"

"I hope there won't be, but I don't aim to take no chances. Now, soon as you can get that man for me, we'll get started and see how much of a job it's going to be to safen up your wheat beds."

"This is just about the right time of day for us to be getting here, Shawahawaki," Longarm remarked to his companion. "Another hour or so and it'll be dark enough for us to get close enough to hear what they're talking about. Whatever sort of tricks they got in mind, we'll start out with a big jump on 'em if we know what they're figuring to do."

Longarm and the Papago who'd come with him were stretched belly-down on the rocky ground that bordered a broad expanse of brownish yellow prairie. They'd topped the rise in the generally level land only moments earlier. Longarm had not expected to see the roof of the building that had suddenly seemed to rise out of the vast expanse of barren land they'd been riding over since leaving the mesa, for it seemed to stretch as far as their eyes could see.

There was still a gap between the bottom rim of the setting sun and the jagged line of the horizon, but the hue of the sun was changing rapidly. Its daytime glare of eye-blasting brilliance was now giving way at the bottom of the orb, turning it slowly into a deeper hue, orange rather than sparkling burnished brass.

When he'd noticed the squared shape of the building that had so suddenly appeared from nowhere to break the sunset skyline, Longarm had signaled his companion to halt. On seeing the building's roof the Papago had pulled up at once. He followed Longarm's example, dismounting quickly and freeing the reins of his horse to trail and keep the animal standing. He followed Longarm's lead, dropping flat and belly-crawling to the edge of the rise. Lying flat on the hot sandy soil, they'd found themselves looking down into the huge crater of some long-extinct volcano.

Between Longarm and Shawahawaki and the point at which the earth and sky merged, most of the land in the huge, roughly circular depression was barren. From the place where Longarm had chosen to stop and watch the land sloped gently downward, then rose in the same circular slope.

Just a bit short of the center of the big dimple in the ground rose the blocky form of a large flat-roofed two-story adobe building. It dominated the other smaller buildings that huddled close to it. These were a long

132

narrow frame building that Longarm knew at first sight could only be a bunkhouse, and another sloped-roof frame building with the broad swinging doors that identified it as a stable.

Almost hidden behind the largest of the group was another building, its end barely visible. The smaller structure was already in the deep shadow of the crater, while the top of the biggest one was still outlined in silhouette against the pre-sunset sky. A pole corral enclosed the area beyond the buildings where horses stood or ambled about aimlessly.

On the land that sloped away from the point where Longarm and Shawahawaki were stretched flat along the rim of the shallow depression, there were bandana-sized patches of thin wispy grass, its yellow stems appearing to be translucent in the pre-sunset light. Fewer in number and even more widely scattered were the clumps of yucca, their knobby stalks rising from sagging sword-shaped leaves that drooped to the rocky soil. Except for the sparse grass patches and yucca stalks the ground was barren.

"I guess that'd be the place we're looking for," Longarm said. "There sure ain't too many ranches hereabouts."

Shawahawaki shook his head. "There are none but those of the Barnes man. But I cannot be sure, for it has been built since I last came this way."

"How long ago was that?"

"Two years or more," the Papago replied.

Longarm said thoughtfully, "Well, somebody sure as hell lives in it, and it's just about got to be where that Rusty Barnes fellow hangs out."

"There does not seem to be anyone there now."

"Take a closer look," Longarm suggested. "Now and

again you can see a little bitty string of smoke coming up from that shed or whatever the building is that we can't see behind that big house. I figure it's got to be the cookshack"

"But there are no men around!"

"They might be around, but doing some work at a place where we can't see 'em," Longarm pointed out.

"I can get close to them without them seeing me," Shawahawaki told Longarm. "Perhaps that is what I should do, so we will be sure."

"We're sure enough right now," Longarm said. "I figure the best thing for us to do is—"

He broke off as a noise like the short muffled tooting of a distant muted trumpet reached them. A moment later the sound was repeated, though it seemed to come from a greater distance. In a few minutes there was a small cacophony of similar sounds. When they died away, a few of the original noises still reached their ears.

"Them's steers blatting," Longarm told his companion. "But I don't guess there's ever been any herds of steers close enough for you to've got acquainted with 'em."

"There is not enough grass or water for us to keep cattle on our mesa," Shawahawaki said slowly. "The Navajo people have sheep on their reservation to the north. But the cattle herds on the ranches of your people are much further away, where we do not travel."

"Well, now, hearing them steers answers a lot of questions I been asking myself," Longarm observed. He was talking to himself as much as to the Papago. "It's just about like I figured it'd be. This Rusty Barnes is aiming to set himself up a ranch down here. He's got to have water if he runs cattle, and he's going to need to

134

make rangeland so they'll have feed. That's why he's been trying to tear up them little patches of wheat you folks grow in the Gila."

"Do you think we can stop him?" Shawahawaki asked. "We cannot do without our wheat, Longarm. If we do not have it, we will starve."

"I reckon we can figure out a way to settle his hash," Longarm said. "The way Judge Hayden explained the law to me, you and your people have got rights to all the water that runs in the Gila along the border of your reservation. Seeing as that's the law, it's my job to see it's kept."

By this time the blatting of the cattle had grown closer. Now and then they could hear the voice of men calling out, but the distance was still too great for them to make out the words of the shouts that were being exchanged. Then men's raised voices drew their attention back to the buildings.

Longarm and Shawahawaki turned their eyes toward the big adobe house in time to see two men appear around the adobe. They carried a big steaming cauldron between them. A third man followed, toting a bucket in each hand. Even at a distance Longarm recognized him as Rusty Barnes. The trio was moving quickly away from the buildings and had gotten perhaps a hundred yards beyond them when Barnes raised his voice.

"This place here's all right," he called to the men who were carrying the big cauldron. "Just set the pot down and go back after that pile of scrap wood I had you put aside when we were mending the corral. We'll need a fire to keep this pot hot. It's going to be a while before those men with the herd are ready to eat. They'll be busy for a while getting the steers settled down for the night."

"That fellow giving the orders is the man we've come looking for," Longarm told his companion. "Calls himself Rusty Barnes. I tangled with him the other day. He's the one that owns this spread here, the one that's been giving you trouble."

"Will you go and talk with him, then?"

Longarm shook his head. "Not just yet. You heard what he said, he's waiting for them steers we've been hearing, and a bunch of steers don't move unless there's men driving 'em. Let's just wait and see how many of 'em there are before we do anything that's apt to start a ruckus."

By this time the figures of two mounted men had come into view at the rim of the sink. In spite of the distance that still lay between the men and Longarm, he could read their gestures. One of the riders was pointing toward the clump of buildings, and after a moment his companion turned his horse and started back. He disappeared below the horizon. The other man kept moving in the direction of the buildings.

"There'll be more'n them two we see now with that cattle herd," Longarm told Shawahawaki. "It looks to me like we're gonna have a mite more on our plate than we'd figured on. What we got to do now is work out how we're going to spoon it up without spilling too much of it."

"When they get here, there will be many more men than we had expected to find," Shawahawaki said.

"Oh, sure," Longarm agreed. "And from the way they sound, them steers is moving along at a pretty good clip. I'd imagine they're close enough to the river now to smell the water, and if they've been driven very far they're bound to be right thirsty."

Even as Longarm was speaking the rider who'd remained at the crest of the dimple raised himself in his stirrups and gestured with a sweep of his arm. His motion was unmistakable, he was ordering the men driving the herd to chouse the steers into a faster pace. A few minutes later the horns and bobbing heads of the first animals broke the line of the horizon, and soon they were streaming over the hump into the hollow at a brisk pace. Longarm tried to count them, but there were too many and they were too scattered to make a tally.

Movement from the cluster of buildings caught their eyes. While they'd been watching the steers, Barnes had started for the barn. In a moment he came out leading a horse, mounted, and headed toward the riders at the head of the herd. Longarm and his companion followed his progress with their eyes as he reached the men with the steers, then a long discussion with many gestures followed.

There was still too great a distance between Barnes's men and Longarm for him to hear what they were saying. Their confab lasted for several minutes before Barnes turned his horse and started back. Instead of heading for the clump of buildings he turned his mount toward the men who'd now returned to the cauldron and were starting a fire under it.

Even before he reached his destination, Barnes called, "I imagine it'll be a while before this bunch that's just come in is ready for supper. They want to get the steers bedded down."

"Then I guess you'll want us to stay here and keep the stew hot?" one of the men at the cauldron asked.

"That's a job one man can handle," Barnes replied. "Cookie, you stay here and feed the fire. Nobby, you come along with me and we'll go lend a hand to them fellows that just got here. I might need some backup, because right now I don't see eye-to-eye with 'em."

"What's the trouble, Rusty?" Nobby asked.

"They say the steers need water. They've been counting on driving 'em to the river, and I kept telling 'em that they wouldn't get there before dark."

"But they don't feel like listening to you? Even when you told 'em they couldn't?"

"No, damn it! What riles me most is I gave them fools orders when I was down at the border hiring 'em on! They was supposed to get here early, but they lally-gagged around and didn't make it! Now it's too late for 'em to get to the river before dark, and any jackass knows you can't drive cattle at night!"

"Hell, boss, they're bound to know it's likely them steers is going to act up if the herd ain't watered before they're bedded down," Nobby replied.

"They don't know what they're asking for! If we bed them critters down at the river they're going to scatter in the dark unless every man jack of us stays up and rides night herd! I tried to tell 'em that, but they wasn't about to listen to me."

"What're you aiming to do, then?"

"Go back and give 'em another tongue-lashing!" Barnes said angrily. "But I want you with me. That bunch is border scum and they'd as soon throw down on a man as look at him."

"I'll have to go down to the stable and get my horse. Lucky I didn't unsaddle when we came in."

"I'll start back, you catch up with me," Barnes told Nobby. "Slim can take care of the stewpot with Cookie when he comes back with more wood."

Nobby started toward the stable and Barnes reined his horse around to rejoin the new arrivals. Longarm and the Papago watched him. He reached the point men who'd been riding at the head of the steers and reined up beside them. Then the three began what soon became obvious was a heated discussion.

Though the distance was too great for the words passed between them to reach Longarm, he could make a fairly accurate guess as to the subject being discussed. Time after time one or another of the men who'd been riding point waved in the general direction of the Gila, and each time the rancher shook his head and swept his arms to indicate the parched and almost barren area of the sloping ground beyond the cluster of houses.

"What I make outa watching them fellows is that the men that came in with the steers ain't about to change their minds none about driving that herd to the river," Longarm remarked to the Papago.

"Which of them is right?"

"I'd say that sorta depends on how far the critters have been driven today," Longarm replied. "You'd know better'n me if there's any graze or water in the direction they came from."

"There is little of either between here and the border of Mexico," Shawahawaki said. "Only cactus plants and a few small water holes."

"Them steers are bound to be hurting for water, then," Longarm said thoughtfully. He was studying the cattle that by now were spreading over the opposite side of the downsloping crater. "And from what you just said they'll be getting awful hungry, too. Right now they look like they're restless as a cat on a hot tin roof, and they're gonna be a lot feistier if they don't get to water real soon."

While Longarm and Shawahawaki were talking the cattle had been pouring over the crater's lip without interruption. By now two more horsemen had ridden into the crater with the steers. They had joined the three who were still in their saddles a short distance from the on-coming cattle, their argument obviously continuing un-abated.

At last the discussion ended. Barnes and the man with the new arrivals, whom Longarm was by now rea-sonably sure he'd tagged as being in charge of the herd, had drawn close together. They were sitting their horses, watching the trail drivers trying to gather the milling steers into a compact herd. The blatting of the animals and the shouts of the riders chousing them were louder than ever now as the trail wranglers worked.

Longarm glanced at the sky. The sun had set while the wrangle between Barnes and the new arrivals was going on. Now the last brightness of its rays were fad-ing fast as the quick-settling darkness began taking the desert country.

Turning to Shawahawaki, Longarm said, "I got an idea them fellows and Barnes are going to be doing a lot of talking when they finally get them steers settled down and go have supper. I aim to be where I can hear 'em, but we need to know what that cattle herd looks like."

"While you wait and listen, I can be your eyes," the Papago suggested.

"Let's do it that way, then," Longarm agreed. "We can't do much till it gets dark. They'll be settling down to eat pretty soon, and when they do I'll sorta wiggle up to where I can listen. Then we can figure out what we'll do next ourselves."

Chapter 12

Longarm wriggled again as he tried to find a position on the stone-hard ground that would be a little less uncomfortable. In the deep blackness that had taken over the land within a few minutes after the sun had set he'd belly-crawled to the dubious shelter of a clump of withered yucca plants.

Longarm had waited until darkness was full before starting his approach. By that time the man called Slim had returned to rekindle the dying fire and set the big cauldron on it. Then he'd taken out a stack of tin plates from the bag that had been brought from the ranch house earlier. Then several of the men who'd driven the herd in had straggled up to the blaze, and finally Rusty Barnes had joined the group.

Studying them in the flickering light of the slim tongues of flame that occasionally shot up to bathe the sides of the iron cauldron, Longarm did not like what he was seeing. To a man they had the look of hard cases, and after a few minutes of conversation they'd proven to Longarm's satisfaction that they were as hardened as they appeared to be.

Barnes had obviously convinced the trail drivers that he was right in demanding that the cattle stay in the valley overnight.

"I've got something in mind for those Mexican steers besides finishing them off to sell for beef," he was saying when Longarm first got within earshot. "And I don't give a damn if we lose a few doing it."

"Maybe you better tell us what it is," one of the hard cases by the fire suggested. "Me and the boys has done everything you paid us to do. We sneaked your herd across the border and choused 'em up here. Far as I'm concerned, our job's finished."

"We'll argue about that later, George," Barnes said. "But I'll tell you right now, I don't mind paying you and your men a little bit more'n we settled on if you'll finish this job the way I want it done."

"Go ahead and lay it out, then," the man called George told him. "We're listening."

"What I want you men to do tomorrow," Barnes continued, "is to trail that herd up north a ways. You'll have to keep the critters away from the river until we get upstream to where the redskins have got a pretty good stand of wheat that's just beginning to come ripe."

"How close is it to the river?" one of the men asked when Barnes paused to take a breath. "Them half-wild Mexican steers can smell water from five or ten miles off. Once they get a whiff of fresh water, they start running for it, then it's the devil's own job trying to turn 'em."

"That's right," George seconded the man quickly. "They're thirsty enough to be mean right now. That's why I'm aiming to set my boys on double watches tonight, so we can hold 'em if they make a bolt for the river. By the time we keep them steers away from the river all night, they'll be mad and mean when we form 'em up and set out tomorrow morning. We'll be fighting 'em all the way."

"You'll get them to where I want them if you know your job," Barnes snapped. "And when you get the critters where I tell you to take 'em, close enough to the Gila to run for water, then your job's done and you can let 'em run all they feel like."

"Not that it's any of my business," one of the men broke in, "but why in hell would you let them steers founder theirselves after you've paid us to drive 'em all this way?"

"Seeing as the job's so close to being finished, I don't mind telling you," Barnes replied. "Them damn Papagos have got a crop of wheat growing in the river. I want those steers turned loose on it so they'll tear it up."

"Did I hear you right?" one of the other outlaws asked. "Are you saying there's wheat growing in the river?"

"Oh, you heard right," Barnes assured him. "That's just exactly what I told you."

"Damn it, mister, I come from Kansas where we grow wheat, and I never seen no stalks sprout out of a riverbed up there."

"I've put in some time in a Kansas wheatfield myself, when I was growing up," Barnes told the man. "I didn't believe it either, the first time I saw it. But if you keep your eyes open tomorrow you'll sure see it for yourself."

"This is the damnedest job I ever taken on," George said, breaking the silence that had followed Barnes's promise. "First you hire me and my boys down in Mexico to rustle them steers and sneak 'em across the border. Then we get 'em here thirsty and you stop us from letting 'em get to the river. Now you want us to push 'em upstream and turn 'em loose on a crop of wheat that's growing in the middle of a river. What's the sense to it?"

"You ain't changed a bit since we was riding together with Sam Bass's bunch down in Texas," Barnes said to George. "Always worrying about a reason for doing a

143

job! No wonder Sam was ready to tell you to go out and dig a hole and pull it closed over you!"

"Yes, and it wasn't too long after that when Sam got careless and got punctured so bad it killed him!" George's voice was sharp as he retorted to Barnes's comment. "So he's pushing up daisies now, and I'm still alive!"

"Don't give yourself too much credit!" Barnes snapped. "If you and some of the others had stuck with Sam, you could've beat off them Rangers that killed him."

"Look who's talking!" George grimaced, then stopped short, shrugged and said, "All that's passed and gone now, Rusty, and there ain't no way to go backward. Let's stop this slanging each other and you tell me what's the sense of this rigamarole you've got laid out for us to do."

"Why, it's as plain as one–two–three," Barnes answered. "I want the Papagos' wheat puddles wiped out, and I don't want to get blamed for it."

"I guess I don't follow you," George said, his voice showing his puzzlement.

"Why, if a rancher new in this place was to be moving a herd of half-wild Mexican steers," Barnes went on, "and them steers was to panic and stampede and mess up the little ponds the Papagos have strung out downstream in the river to grow their wheat in, the rancher couldn't rightly be blamed for an accident like that, could he?"

George said nothing for a moment, then he loosed a loud guffaw that brought half his men to their feet in surprise. When his laughter had subsided, the outlaw turned to Barnes, still chuckling and shaking his head.

"I got to hand it to you, Rusty," he said. "All this time I been thinking you was a little bit tetched in the head. I tried my damnedest to figure out why the hell you'd take the trouble to go all the way down to the border and chouse me out with the old Mexican grapevine just to put a herd of half-wild steers together and drive it up here when you could've got better range stock a lot closer. But I got the idea, now."

"I guess it does seem like I've taken a lot of trouble," Barnes told him. "But I aim to stay here a while. A man gets edgy when he's on the dodge too much."

"And so you want the folks in Arizona Territory to figure you're a nice, tame rancher," George said. "Well, I don't know. Maybe you got the right idea."

"I thought so, too"—Barnes nodded—"but now there's some snoopy federal marshal nosying around, trying to help the damn redskins!"

"You figure the Papagos won't use the river anymore, if you tear their playhouse down?" George asked.

"Why, hell's bells, they won't have much choice," Barnes shot back. "And I don't want anybody pointing their fingers at me, so I figured out that the easiest way to get the water I need to turn this place into a fine ranch is to stop the Papagos from using the water I need myself."

George was silent for a moment, then he nodded slowly. "I guess when you put it that way, it does make sense. All right, Rusty. Fifty dollars more a man and a hundred for me, and we'll take on the extra job."

"Now, that's a goddamned holdup!" Barnes protested. "Half of that's more like what it'd be worth to me!"

"Go ahead and do it yourself, then!" George snapped. "Me and my boys can make a lot more with a lot less trouble. We'd as lief as not saddle up and ride outa here at daybreak if you're gonna turn skinflint on us."

"I didn't say I wouldn't pay it!" Barnes replied quickly. "But I'd say yes a lot quicker if you'll settle for half that much. I'm just getting this spread going, and the chances are I'll have some more work you and your bunch can do before I've got things here fixed up the way I want 'em to be."

"Thirty and sixty, then."

"Deal!" Barnes nodded. "I'll add it to what you got coming when I pay off the other half of what we settled for when we struck up this deal in Mexico."

"I'll remind you, if it slips your mind," George promised. "Now let's get on with supper. It's going to be a long night, because every man jack of us is going to have to ride herd till daybreak. Them steers is edgy as all hell and they can smell water from a long ways off. If they start towards the river, it's going to take all of us to hold 'em here."

When he saw George stand up and the other men beginning to start toward the pot to replenish their plates, Longarm decided that he'd heard enough. He began edging away, keeping his eyes fixed on the men around the fire and moving backward by digging his boot toes into the hard ground, snaking back toward the spot where he'd left the Papagos waiting.

He'd covered only a few yards and was about to rise in order to move faster when a shadow rose from the ground close beside him and he felt the cold muzzle of a revolver pressed into his neck just under his jawbone.

"E-stop queek, *hombre*," the man he'd taken for a shadow commanded. "*Mi pistola* ees cock. Eef you move, I am e-pull the treeger."

Longarm had been in enough tight squeezes to be able to judge instantly just how tight this one was. There was a menace in the Mexican's words that warned him the man meant exactly what he said. He remained motionless while he felt his Colt being yanked from its holster, but in his

146

mind he was swearing at himself for having been so careless and allowing himself to be seen and captured.

"Now you weel e-stand up," the man who held the pistol commanded. "Then we weel e-go down to the fire and e-see who you are and what you do here."

With the Mexican's pistol jabbed firmly into his spine, Longarm had no choice but to obey. He started walking toward the fire, his mind working faster than his legs. Most of the men around the fire had started eating their second helping, but one of them looked up and saw Longarm and the man who'd captured him approaching.

"Hey, look there!" he called. "That's Pancho, and damned if he ain't caught somebody snooping!"

"I am see heem e-sneak up to leesten," Pancho said. "So I am e-sneak up behind heem." He handed Longarm's Colt to George. "I am e-take thees. Eef you keel heem, I want eet back."

"I'll see you get it," George promised. "Now let's get him up to the fire so's we can see who he is. There's one sure thing, he ain't got no business being here, or he wouldn't be skulking around the way you said he was."

Longarm did not resist as Pancho prodded him close to the blaze. Even before his face was lighted by the dying fire under the cauldron, one of the men in the group that was crowding up called out, "Hell, I know this son of a bitch! He's that damn U.S. marshal they call Longarm!"

"You sure about that?" George asked.

"Sure enough to bet you a dollar to a plugged nickel that if you go through his pockets you'll find a marshal's badge with his name on it."

"Take a look, George," Barnes said. He turned away long enough to say, "Somebody toss another chunk or two of wood on the fire so we can see what we're

147

doing." Then, swiveling back to face Pancho and Long-arm, he said, "Pancho, bring that fellow up closer to the fire. I think he's that fella who shot Ed Cole!"

Longarm's captor pushed him in the direction of the revived blaze. George stepped up to Longarm and began poking into his pockets. Longarm said nothing. His eyes were fixed on George's face for the few moments required by the outlaw to reach the pocket in which Long-arm carried the wallet containing his badge. Fishing out the wallet, the man flipped it open.

"Damned if you didn't call it, Pants!" he said over his shoulder to the man who'd identified Longarm. "Custis Long's the name on this badge. We sure have got Longarm, all right."

His voice flat and expressionless, Longarm said quietly, "Getting me and holding on to me are two different things, George. You might say we're even, because I got you, too. I've looked at your face on a lot of Wanted posters, and I make you out to be George Caspar. Robbed a U.S. Mail coach over in Texas."

"Now, how in—" George began.

Barnes cut him short. "That's enough palaver! Can't you see he's trying to get you rattled?"

"I guess you're right," Caspar agreed. "And he was damned close to doing it! But what the hell are we going to do with him, now that we've got him?"

"Don't worry," Barnes replied. "We'll figure out a way to get rid of him. We've got a job on our hands right now, and we better finish it before we start worrying about Longarm."

"Don't be in a hurry on my account," Longarm said. His words were unhurried, almost casual, as he said, "But if I was you, I'd stop and think twice before you go ahead and try to finish up this job you've got schemed up. You men are going to have enough charges against you to put you away for a long time, when I take you in."

"Now, damn you, Longarm!" Caspar burst out. "You've got the gall to stand there and—"

Barnes cut him off again. "Shut up!" he snapped. "Longarm nor nobody else is going to take us in, not if we keep cool and get on with our business!"

"Seems to me the most important business we've got right this minute is Longarm," Caspar observed.

"Damned if it is!" Barnes exploded. "My steers come first! I didn't hire you to drive that herd up from Mexico just to keep the grass off my range!"

"Now, don't get all riled up," Caspar said quickly. "We'll do the job you wanted, just like I said we would."

"While we're talking about that, you and your bunch better get back to that herd," Barnes told him. "If you don't keep those wild steers bunched tonight, you'll waste half of tomorrow forming 'em up again, and I want to start out early."

George Caspar had regained his composure by this time. He said, "You're right, Rusty." Turning to the others he said, "You men hit the leather. The sooner you get back to the herd, the less trouble we'll have bunching 'em up at daybreak."

"You'll be coming with us, I guess?" one of the men asked.

"Soon as I get through talking to Rusty," George promised.

There were a few grumbles from the men who stood around the dying fire, but they started trickling off through the darkness. Within a few minutes only Barnes and Caspar and Longarm remained, standing beside the small bed of fading coals.

"We've got this son of a bitch on our hands now,"

Barnes said to Caspar. "And from what I've heard, he's as slippery as they come. If we want to keep him around very long, the first thing we'd better do is tie him up."

"What with?" George asked. "I don't want to use my lariat, and that's—" He stopped and shook his head, then went on, "I guess I'm losing my edge, Rusty. Hold on to him while I go get a saddle string. That'll keep him tamed."

Stepping over to his horse, Caspar opened his jackknife and lopped off a saddle string. He brought the narrow strip of leather back and came to a stop behind Longarm.

"If you know what's good for you, you'll put your arms around here and stand still while I tie you up," he said.

Longarm had heard the chill of death in an adversary's voice too many times not to recognize it when Caspar spoke. He brought down his arms and held them behind his back while the outlaw looped the leather strip around his wrists and tied it. Then Caspar stepped away and went back to stand beside Barnes.

"That's better," Barnes said. "I don't see but one thing that we can do with him. Do you?"

Shaking his head, Caspar replied, "Nope. We'll have to get rid of him, and I won't mind doing the job. You want me to take care of it now?"

"No, damn it!" Barnes exclaimed. "I don't know the first thing about any of those men you hired on to get my steers up from Mexico. What do you think would happen if one of them got drunk and began bragging about how he helped put Longarm away?"

"That hadn't occurred to me," Caspar admitted.

"Would you trust 'em to keep quiet?"

"Hell, Rusty, I don't know those fellows much better than you do! They're just a bunch I picked up in saloons and outlaw hidey-holes down in Mexico."

"That's about how I figured it," Barnes said. "Long-

150

arm works out of Denver, and somebody there's going to start asking questions if they don't hear from him sooner or later."

Longarm was quick to grasp the opening Barnes had given him. In a quietly assured voice he said, "If you two know what's good for you, you'll cut my hands free and give up."

"Like hell we will!" Caspar told him. "You're not going to be alive long enough to see the sun come up!"

"Now, I know you'd like to figure on that," Longarm told him, his voice still calm and assured. "But your friend there hit the nail square on the head a minute ago. If I don't report back to my office in Denver inside of a day or so, you can figure out what's going to happen."

"Shut up, damn you!" Caspar snapped. "You're not going to talk us into doing anything! Or not doing anything, whichever way you want to put it!"

"Both of you shut up!" Barnes commanded. "While you've been wasting time jabbering, I've been thinking." He turned to Caspar and said, "I want that herd of steers up at those Papago water holes tomorrow. And I don't trust that bunch you hired on down in Mexico mixed up in this business with Longarm."

"That's easy enough for you to say," Caspar retorted. "But I don't hear you coming up with any scheme for us to use."

"All I know is that Longarm's got to be killed."

"You've got that much of it thought out, then?"

"As best I can." Barnes nodded. "Him popping up out of nowhere's thrown my whole plan out of kilter. I don't aim to kill the son of a bitch where you or anybody else can see me pull the trigger. Now, you cut off another saddle string and we'll tie his feet."

151

"You ain't figuring on leaving him here!" Caspar objected.

"I don't see why not. By the time we get to where you left those Mexican steers and bunch 'em up again, it'll be about the right time to head 'em up the river. Then I'll pay off you and your crew and you can head back to where you came from."

"And you'll be here by yourself to get rid of Longarm?"

"That's about the size of it," Barnes said. "The less anybody but me knows what happens to Longarm after that, the better I'm going to like it. Now, shake a leg and tie his feet, and we'll be on our way."

Longarm did not struggle when Caspar lashed his feet together, nor did he say anything. He lay quietly beside the fading coals while Barnes and Caspar mounted and rode away, leaving him bound and helpless.

Chapter 13

Knowing as he did how the minds of criminals work, Longarm did not move until he was sure that Barnes and Caspar had not stopped a short distance away to watch him, in case he tried to escape. He lay quietly, testing the darkness with his ears by turning his head slowly, almost imperceptibly. He knew that to anyone watching from the darkness the faint glow that still radiated from the almost dead fire made him highly visible and a very vulnerable target.

When he was sure that the entire group had indeed left him alone, Longarm finally began to test his bonds. The leather thongs that secured his feet remained tight when he spread his knees and tried to force some slack into them. This did not bother him too greatly, for his calf-high boots kept the thin strips from biting into his flesh. The binding on his arms was an entirely different matter, for the thongs that held his wrists immobilized had been pulled very, very tight.

When he stretched his elbows away from his torso and started to flex his forearms the narrow piece of rawhide securing his wrists grew tighter instantly. As he strained his muscles the leather cut cruelly into skin and flesh and compressed the sensitive nerves covered only by a thin layer of skin. He had to relax the pressure at once, and two facts popped into his mind instantly: The first was that it would be impossible for him to slip his hands out of the binding; the second was that unless he achieved what at the moment seemed impossible his hands would soon swell and become useless.

Relaxing as best he could in his uncomfortable position, Longarm twisted his head around. He peered through the darkness in the steadily decreasing glow of the dying coals for a stick or twig that he might manage to reach and use as a lever. He abandoned this effort almost at once, realizing that even if he saw something sturdy enough to serve his purpose he would still be unable to twist his fingers into a position to use it.

As he swiveled his head, peering into the gloom, he caught sight of the big cast-iron cauldron that had contained the stew served for supper. It had been dragged off the cooking fire when the last of the outlaws had refilled their plates. He paid little attention to the oversized cooking pot for a moment, then like a flame being lighted with a guttering match the solution to his dilemma flashed into his mind.

Though movement was difficult and at times exasperating, Longarm managed to turn until he was lying on his back. He bent his knees, pulling them up as far as possible, and pushed on the ground with his heels. The push moved him only a few inches, but even that was progress. He pushed again and again, ignoring the rasping of his hands and wrists as they scraped on the dry hard earth.

At first the distance to the tall straight-sided pot seemed endless. He moved inch by inch until his shoulder touched it, and at that point he realized that at least half the battle had been won. He dug his boot

154

heels into the resisting soil, then pushed to straighten out his legs.

His shoulders scraped against the rough iron pot as the pressure of his legs slid them upward. Buttocks on the ground, Longarm leaned back against the pot and pushed again. The heavy cauldron leaned a bit, but did not overturn. Longarm repeated the maneuver, and now he could turn his head and peer down into the pot. The night's sky-shine was reflected in a pool of the stew that remained in the massive vessel.

Bending his knees, Longarm pulled his feet as near to his buttocks as possible and pushed again. The pot shifted another fraction of an inch, but still remained upright. His next upward push brought his bound wrists into contact with the side of the vessel. Ignoring the pain caused by the pressure of his body, which pinned his bound wrists to the pot and scraped his hands on its rough iron side, Longarm pushed once more.

When he felt the rim of the big vessel rasp still more skin off his hands as they rose above its girdling lip, Longarm knew that he had won. He moved his arms backward as far as possible and relaxed his leg muscles until he could feel his hands dipping into the three or four inches of soupy stew that the pot still contained.

Waiting the few moments required for the warm liquid in the vessel to penetrate the untanned leather of the thongs binding his wrists, Longarm stretched his elbows and began working them back and forth. It seemed to him that an infinity of time passed before he could feel the leather soften and stretch, then within a few more seconds the bindings no longer bit into his wrists and he could pull his hands free.

His leg muscles protested as Longarm straightened his knees and stood up. He brought his hands around in

155

front of him. They were scratched and smarting and dripping with the soupy juice that had softened the leather that had bound them, but his fingers were once again moving freely. Ignoring the protests of the strained muscles in his calves and thighs, Longarm dropped to his knees and rubbed his hands in the sparse grass and the dusty soil until he'd removed most of the liquid that was left on them.

"Old son," he said aloud in the darkness, "them hands are going to make it look like you've been trying to break up a fight between two or three wildcats. They'll likely keep on smarting for a pretty good spell, but the main thing is you're just about free and clear and ready to go again."

Once he'd gotten his hands free of sludge and limbered up a bit Longarm began working on the bindings that still held his ankles together. The leg thongs had not been drawn as tightly as those on his arms, and very little time was needed for him to free himself completely. He stood up and flexed the muscles in his arms and legs for several minutes. Slowly, with tinglings and twitches, they returned to normal.

Glancing in the direction of the ranch house, Longarm could not see any lights, nor was there any aura of light coming from a lamp that might be out of his direct line of sight. He knew by now that he'd gained all the night vision that was possible, and that any hint of a light would register on his expanded pupils.

By habit he reached into his vest pocket and took out one of his long thin cigars. He had it clenched between his teeth and was fumbling for a match when the thought struck him that a light where he was standing would be an alarm beacon to any of the outlaws who glanced in his direction. Stepping over to the remnants of the cooking fire, he stirred the still-glowing embers with his boot toe, then hunkered down and bent his head forward until the tip of the long cigar touched the nearest coal and puffed the cigar until it was drawing.

Shielding its glowing tip with one hand, he stood up, puffing luxuriously. He was exhaling the smoke when a tiny sound reached his ears from the darkness. In automatic reflex, Longarm's hand dropped to his empty holster. He moved it instantly to his vest pocket, and felt the little derringer that the outlaw who'd captured him had overlooked. He had the derringer in his hand and was swiveling in the direction of the sound when Shawahawaki's voice broke the night's stillness.

"No, Longarm! It's only me!"

"Damned if you can't sneak up quiet on a man!" Longarm exclaimed, lowering the derringer.

"I circled around to make sure there was no one hidden close by," Shawahawaki explained. "As I was getting close, it occurred to me that the other men might be using you as bait in a trap to catch me."

"I don't figure they even thought there might be somebody with me," Longarm said. "That Barnes fellow was in an all-fired hurry to get his bunch back to that herd of steers."

"I heard them coming," Shawahawaki told him. "And when I got close enough to this place to see the little fire glow, I stopped and tethered my horse in the little canyon with yours. Tell me, Longarm, what has happened?"

"I wasn't minding what I was doing, like a damn fool," Longarm replied. "And I got caught. Then Barnes and his men left to go bunch them wild Mexican steers. They'll be riding herd on 'em till its daybreak,

157

then they aim to drive 'em up to them patches of wheat you folks have got growing in the Gila."

"They intend to turn the cattle into our wheat patches?"

"A little bit worse'n that, Shawahawaki. Them steers ain't been watered or grazed since yesterday evening. The way Barnes figures it, the critters are going to be so thirsty and hungry by the time they get to your little wheat ponds that they'll trample 'em all to smithereens."

Shawahawaki was silent for a moment, then he said, "Yes, I am sure that is what the steers would do. And it takes many years to prepare the riverbed for wheat. Our people would go hungry for many years if the river ponds were ruined."

"Do you reckon your folks could stop a bunch of wild steers that's half starved and mean as all sin?"

"No," the Papago replied unhesitatingly. "We do not have enough guns to stop a herd of wild cattle."

"Then it looks to me like the only thing we can do is keep them steers from starting out," Longarm said.

"But how can we do that? There are only two of us."

"Sure," Longarm agreed. "And Barnes has got maybe a dozen or more men. But them odds ain't too bad, Shawahawaki. Let's start back to where we hid our horses. Daylight won't get here for quite a spell. We can do some thinking on the way, and maybe we'll come up with something."

Although both Longarm and Shawahawaki were well aware that they had only the time remaining until dawn to solve their problem, they started walking through the starlit darkness at an easy pace toward the small canyon where their horses were concealed. They moved through the night in silence, each of them trying to think of a plan that would enable them to overcome the odds they faced. They'd covered perhaps half the distance to the canyon when Longarm stopped short.

Shawahawaki stopped when Longarm did and asked, "Why are we stopping, Longarm? We are not even near our horses yet."

"Sure, I know that. But I've been thinking just like you have and all of a sudden it came to me that we've been missing a bet."

"What do you mean?" the Papago asked.

"A while back we were cudgeling our brains about a way to stop them outlaws from ruining your wheat beds, and I guess sorta feeling bad because we couldn't come up with any sort of scheme."

"And now you have one?"

"Not exactly," Longarm replied. "But it just came to me that we never will figure out a plan unless we know what we got to plan around."

"I do not understand."

"It might be that I don't, either. But back there where them fellows had supper, there's a big house and a barn. Far as I know, there ain't nobody in either place. They're all out riding night herd on them Mexican steers."

"I still do not understand," Shawahawaki said. His voice was puzzled and questioning at the same time.

"What I'm getting at is that there's always stuff in a ranch's barn, old bits and pieces of things that's been put aside because a man never knows what he might need. Tools and—well, I been in a few barns in my day, and I just bet if we go look in the one back there we're likely to find something that'd give us an idea for a plan."

"You are saying we should go back and look? Even without knowing what we might find?"

"That's what I'm aiming at," Longarm replied. "But let's go on and get our horses first. Then we'll mosey back and have a look-see in that barn."

Longarm reined in a short distance from the structures that rose ahead of them in the starlit darkness. Beside him, Shawahawaki also brought his horse to a halt. They looked at the three buildings for a moment, searching in vain for any signs of life. There were none, and the pole corral which was barely visible beyond the buildings was empty.

"There sure ain't nobody around here," Longarm said. Even though the evidence of his eyes had told him this from the beginning, there was a tone of relief in his voice.

He made no effort to go closer to the buildings, but sat in his saddle, studying them. The adobe house which Longarm had glimpsed earlier was much larger than he'd taken it to be, rising two stories above the ground. All its windows were dark black rectangles that broke the monotony of its walls. Beyond it the structure that had been hidden by the house now showed as a low elongated rectangle. Its shape told him that it was probably a cookhouse. Still further away the third building glittered metallically. It was a big barn, obviously fairly new, for its sides of corrugated sheet iron still gleamed in pristine luster, even in the darkness.

"That's the one we need to head for," Longarm told the Papago. "It catches all the odds and ends nobody needs right now but're too good to throw away."

Although their eyes had become accustomed to the starlit dimness of the desert night, the blackness that

160

shrouded them when they entered the big rambling barn was even darker. Both Longarm and Shawahawaki halted just inside the door and blinked as they tried to peer through the midnight shroud of its interior. Then their night vision adjusted to the greater darkness and they could make out the empty stalls that ran along both sides of the huge structure, and the amorphous shapes of the bags and bundles and unidentifiable objects that were piled in heaps that filled the center of the dirt floor.

"That's the stuff we better look over," Longarm said. "I ain't got no more idea than an old horse what all might be in that pile of truck in the middle, but I figure there's maybe a half chance we'll run across something that we can use."

"Can you tell me what we are looking for?"

"I wish I could, Shawahawaki. Fact of the matter is, I don't rightly know myself what we might find in that litter that'd help us corral a herd of half-wild Mexican steers."

"I will ask as we go along, then," the Papago said. The tone of his voice showed how puzzled he was.

"You go down on one side of this truck, I'll take the other one," Longarm told him. "We'll just mosey along, and if we don't see anything turn up that strikes our fancy, we'll just have to go face down them scoundrels."

They began moving slowly along, with Longarm striking a match now and then, holding it high to cast a feeble light on the heap of miscellany. The items they saw gave no signs of being useful in their efforts to halt a herd of steers. Most of the heaped-up discards had long outlived their usefulness, but Longarm knew that on isolated ranches virtually nothing that might possibly be reused was ever thrown away.

161

They encountered short lengths of broken rope, wads of tired, frayed rags, buckets of bent and rusted nails, dented cooking pots, a broken chair or two, a couple of chamber pots with jagged vees in their broad lips, an old saddle with badly torn and weathered leather, a few short planks of mixed boards and two-by-fours, a few heaps of cracked cups and plates and other crockery, as well as a few boards nailed together by some ham-handed cowhand who'd started to make a shelf or some other small convenience and abandoned the project before finishing it.

Longarm had struck a half-dozen matches as they moved slowly along, and they were nearing the end of the piles when he struck a fresh match. Its flame when the match head flared up glinted back from the floor with the dull sheen of metallic grey in the sudden burst of brilliance. Longarm took another step ahead, holding the match higher to spread its rays more widely. Then he stopped and lowered the hand that held the burning match. His mind began churning with the birth of an idea, and he held the match until it began burning his fingers.

"Hold up a minute, Shawahawaki!" he exclaimed, dropping the match and quickly striking another. "I think maybe we found what we need, even if we didn't know it was in here or that it was what we were looking for."

"What is it, then?" Shawahawaki asked, stepping up to bring himself across from Longarm.

"Barbwire," Longarm replied. "There's four, maybe five rolls laying here. Some of its been used pretty good and a little bit of it's new, and I ain't sure it's enough to handle the idea that just popped into my mind. But it's the only thing we've run across that we might use to

162

help us, and if ever we needed some help, now's the time."

On the other side of the junk pile Shawahawaki had stopped opposite Longarm. He bent to look, but Longarm's fresh match was already burning low and the flame reached his fingers before he realized how long he'd been holding it. He flicked the match out and struck another by dragging his thumbnail across its head.

"You have thought of a way to help us with this wire?" the Papago asked.

"Maybe. If there's enough of it," Longarm answered.

He was prodding at the coils of wire with the toe of his boot as he spoke. When they'd been separated and lay in tight loops across the barn's dirt floor he lighted another match and hunkered down, peering at each pile in turn to estimate the length of the wire in each one. Shawahawaki bent close to look at the piles.

"Beyond Hayden's Landing I have seen fences made of barbed wire, but they are long, and these pieces we have found are very short," Shawahawaki pointed out. "And to make a fence, we must have posts to put the wire on, this much I know."

"Well, now, the kinda fence I got in mind is sorta different from the ones you've seen," Longarm said. "One post's all we need." Then a thoughtful look spread over Longarm's face and he added, "Or maybe two. And we can cobble them up from some of them pieces of wood over yonder. If we take a few minutes to look around, I'd imagine we can even find a few new posts, and I got to admit they'd come in mighty handy."

Frowning, Shawahawaki asked, "How can we make a fence without posts?"

"You know the old saying," Longarm told him. Then

after a moment's thought he amended his remark, saying, "On second thought, maybe you don't. I ain't sure you Papagos have got a lot of handy little sayings like ours. But the folks back where I grew up used to say that there's more ways to kill a cat then choking it with cream."

While Longarm talked, he was busy piling the thin rolls of barbwire from the clutter that was strewn along the center of the barn and piling them in the space between the ranch's discards and the line of open stalls.

Shawahawaki shook his head as he said, "I still do not see how we can make a fence with nothing but wire."

Longarm said, "Might be I'm sorta stretching things when I call what I got in mind a fence, but you'll see how it works when we find the right place to put it up." He looked around, saw no more rolls of wire, and added, "Now we got to find some kinda wood that we can use for a fence post."

"There are pieces of wood close to the door," the Papago volunteered. "I saw them when we came in."

"Then we'll pick up what we need when we bring one of the horses in to load this wire on. I guess you know how to straddle a horse's rump, don't you?"

"Of course. Our people ride double much of the time because we have so few horses."

"That settles that, then," Longarm told him. "Now let's get the wood pieces we'll need and one of them buckets of nails and go look for a piace to put our fence up. The faster we find it the better, because them outlaws are going to start the steers out here at daybreak, and it's going to take us a little time to get our surprise ready for 'em."

164

Chapter 14

"This place sorta stuck in my head when I came up with this scheme we're going to try," Longarm told Shawahawaki. "I reckon it's about the best stretch we're going to find to try our stunt. At least, I can't think of a better one up ahead."

Longarm had reined in their horses dangerously near the rim of the long deep canyon. As yet the sun had not risen fully, although the false dawn was swiftly being replaced by the gold of sunrise. Only a sliver of the sun's orb was visible, and the beginning of the long desert dawn was lightening the land. They could already see the outlines of the high mesas to the east and that of the more distant river, even though darkness still held sway at the bottom of the canyon where they'd stopped.

A quarter of a mile to the east, beyond the beginning of the canyon, the stretch of arid featureless soil was cut off by the bank of the Gila. The river itself was invisible, for it flowed in a sinuous channel cut through a broad bed of sand at the bottom of a drop-off as steep as the walls of the narrow canyon. In the blunt-ended vee that stretched between the riverbank and the canyon's lip the only growing things were a few thin colorless stalks of yucca.

Longarm and Shawahawaki were riding double, Longarm in the saddle of his horse, the Papago straddling its rump. They were leading Shawahawaki's horse, which bore the load of barbed wire and the three or four long sturdy fence posts they'd finally discovered in the barn of the deserted ranch.

Looking at the jagged edged converging areas of darkness formed by the river on one side and the canyon on the other, Longarm said, "That gully ain't exactly like the one up to the north, but it's wide enough and I guess it'll be deep enough to suit us. And it still ain't too close to them stands of wheat your folks raise for your crop to be hurt none."

"Will we have enough wire to stretch across the land between here and the river?" Shawahawaki asked.

"Likely we can make do. Once them steers are turned, the ones in back are going to play follow the leader, just like all cattle do, whether they're wild or tame."

"Then let us begin our work," the Papago suggested. "From what you told me of hearing last night, the men driving the cattle will be starting soon."

"Oh, we got all the time we're likely to need," Longarm assured him. "It ain't such a much of a job we got to do, but I got a hunch you're right about getting started. We sure ain't got much in the way of tools to work with, and that's apt to slow us down a mite."

Shawahawaki was already sliding off the horse's rump. Longarm levered out of his saddle and started walking up to the rim of the canyon. Shawahawaki matched him stride for stride. They stopped and stood looking down into the canyon. Longarm took out one of his thin cigars and lighted it as they studied the narrow

166

slash with almost vertical walls that cut a zigzagging gully across the arid terrain.

"It's deep enough, all right," he said. "And after they've fallen ass-over-appetite down them steep walls, I don't imagine that even them tough Mexican steers are apt to try climbing out."

"I would say that, too," the Papago agreed. "If the wire is strong enough to turn them."

"Back in the days when I was cowhanding, I never did see a steer that had enough sand in his craw to buck up against barbwire," Longarm said. "Now let's mosey over to the river and see how things are going to stack up on that side. We might as well leave the horses to stand. Nobody's apt to be coming this way until Barnes and his bunch get here."

Crossing the narrow triangular spit of land between the canyon and the riverbank took only a few minutes. They stopped where the bank dropped away in an almost vertical slant to the wide expanse of dry shining golden sand studded here and there by rocks and small boulders. This was the original riverbed, carved out by the Gila River at some long-ago time before the water failed and what had been a green fertile stretch of prairie became a semi-arid desert.

Nothing grew now between the original banks of the river and the shrunken channel in which the Gila now flowed. Gazing at it now, Longarm guessed that he could cross it in four or five strides and without getting water in his calf-high boots. It was one of many Western rivers that were described jokingly as being "a mile wide and two inches deep." The sun was above the mesas by now, reflecting in dancing twinkles on the river's surface.

In its narrow present-day channel the Gila flowed

calmly, though it was three or four times as wide here as it was further downstream, where the Papagos grew their small patches of wheat. Beyond the stream the high mesas thrust up like fortress walls. Their sides were still in shadows now, and their faces were too dark to allow Longarm to make out details, but he had seen enough at his first quick glance to be able to tell that he'd chosen the right spot.

"If I didn't know different, I'd swear this place was just made for us," he told Shawahawaki. "I'll just bet we won't have a mite of trouble getting them steers to behave the way I figure they will."

"We can go to work, then," the Papago suggested.

"Sure. Right away, too," Longarm agreed. Then his memory was jogged and he said, "There's one little job I got to do before we start work, though. I ought to've done it before now, but it's been a while since I heard the right words. I think I got 'em all strung out in the right place now, so we might as well take care of it."

"This thing we must do, I do not understand, Longarm," Shawahawaki said. "Is not the fence our only job?"

"Oh, that's our big job, you're right about that. But I got to thinking while we were on the way here, there ain't much chance of us getting this job finished without some shooting. I aim to swear you in as my legal deputy just in case one of them outlaws is to get killed. That way there ain't nobody going to point no fingers at you."

"I have never killed a man!" the Papago protested. "Not even when I was a wild young buck and ready to fight any time!"

"That was a while back," Longarm reminded his companion. "Things ain't the same as they used to be,

168

Shawahawaki. There's a bunch of damned softheads running around now that must've been let outa the crazy house by mistake. They never have learned that a killer's a killer, and putting him behind bars for a little while ain't going to keep him from killing somebody else."

"You mean that I could be punished for killing a man who is trying to kill me?"

"That's about how it stacks up," Longarm replied. "The law seems to treat Indians that way. But if you're wearing a badge, it ain't likely you'll find yourself in trouble."

"How do you go about this thing, this swearing in?"

"By rights, I guess we oughta have a Bible, but that's something I don't tote with me. Just hold up your right hand, and when I ask the question, you say 'I do.'"

"I do what?"

"What the questions asks," Longarm told him. "It was a long time ago that I learned the right words, but I don't think I've forgotten 'em."

"Go ahead, then," the Indian said.

"Get your right hand up in the air, then," Longarm said. "And when I ask you the question, just say 'I do,' like I told you a minute ago."

Shawahawaki lifted his hand. Longarm lifted his and for a moment found that he could not remember as much of the oath as he'd thought he could earlier. Then he gave up trying and began speaking.

"Do you swear you'll defend the United States against all the enemies you run into . . . and do whatever jobs you get the best way you can?" he said, pausing once or twice as he racked his brain trying to recall the exact phrasing he'd heard so many years ago, when he'd sworn the oath on becoming a U.S. marshal.

"I do," Shawahawaki replied.

"Good enough," Longarm said, letting his arm drop. "Now we can get down to business again."

"That is all there is?"

"All I can recall, but it's all we need. Now you're my official deputy and you got the right to do whatever you need to do to see that folks keep the law. Now, let's go to work and see if we can't settle them outlaws' hash."

As they started back to the horses, Longarm began taking long measured paces and counting them aloud as they moved. Shawahawaki watched him for a short distance and then asked, "Is it important that we know how many paces wide this place is?"

"Maybe not all that much, but it'll help when I start in splicing that barbwire into one piece. It's got to be pretty much just so, with a big fence post in the middle, or this scheme ain't going to work right."

They reached the horses and with Shawahawaki leading one of the animals and Longhorn the other they retraced their steps to the point Longarm had determined to be the center of the vee of solid soil. Longarm scratched an X in the ground with his boot heel and turned to his companion.

"Here's where we get down to the real work," he told Shawahawaki. "Grab hold of that shovel we found in the barn and start digging right in front of that rock ledge, where I made that mark."

"How deep must I dig?"

"Better go down as far as you can while I'm splicing barbwire," Longarm replied. "The hole we need don't have to be very big around, but it needs to be as deep as we can make it and still have about four or five feet of a couple of them stoutest and longest fence posts still sticking up above ground."

170

While Shawahawaki dug, Longarm turned his attention to the coils of barbwire they'd discovered in the ranch barn. He began by unwinding each coil and stretching the spike-studded wire as straight as possible. He laid the straightened wires side by side, then moved to his next task. Working without the aid of tools or gloves, Longarm began splicing the short lengths end-to-end to form a single long strand.

For the first few minutes he swore hard and often as one of the sharp-pointed barbs nicked a fingertip or the back or palm of his hand. As he gained experience and became accustomed to the feel and flex of the wire the nicks were less frequent and the splices neater. He wound the ends of each splice back upon the wire to cover the spot where the two lengths overlapped. Then he looked around until he spotted a big flat stone nearby and used it as an anvil with a fist-sized one as a hammer to pound the splices, and make sure they would not give way. He tested his work by standing on the wire and pulling it upward, watching the splices as he tugged, to be sure that his improvised joints would hold up under stress.

Length by length of wire Longarm's unified strand grew longer. He reached the last joint and finished it, then anchored one end by looping it around the heaviest stone he could find and began dragging the other end over the bare sandy ground to stretch it across the narrowest point in the vee between the riverbed and the canyon.

When he reached the point where Shawahawaki was digging, Longarm stopped and dropped the wire he'd been dragging. His first glance was enough to show him that the Papago had done his best to follow in the instructions he'd been given. He'd excavated the sandy soil to form a deep hole only a bit larger in diameter than the width of the shovel, and almost as deep as the tool's long handle. He was kneeling beside the hole, trying to bring up still another shovelful from its depths when he looked up and saw Longarm.

"Do you think this is deep enough?" he asked.

"Plenty deep, Shawahawaki. There ain't much way you're going to dig it no deeper unless you can stretch that shovel's handle a foot or so longer."

For a moment a puzzled frown flitted across Shawahawaki's bronzed face, then he smiled and said, "You are making a joke at me." Then his smile faded, his face grew serious and he asked, "Now what must we do?"

"Why, we'll set our fence posts solid in the hole and stretch the barbwire up between it and the river on one side and that little canyon on the other side, to make a fence."

While he talked, Longarm had lifted one of the long stout fence posts and was carrying it to the hole. He upended it and let it slide down until it hit bottom. The post leaned slightly askew, protruding in a slant above the desert floor. Shawahawaki watched him with a puzzled frown as he maneuvered the post to lean slightly forward, slanting in the direction from which the herd would be forced to come. Then he added a second post by sliding it into the hole beside the first.

"We have too few fence posts, Longarm," the Papago said. "There are only two more left. How will we hold both ends of the wire?"

"Don't worry, two more's plenty. We'll set them at the end where the river is. Then over at the canyon end there's a big rock spur sticking out just a little ways down the wall. We can loop the end of the barbwire

172

around it." While he talked Longarm was pushing dirt into the hole from the pile beside it.

"Will the fence be strong enough to stop the steers?"

"Not for very long, but you got to remember that them critters ain't never seen a fence before, let alone a barbwire one. I got a real strong hunch that this wire's gonna spook the hell out of 'em, and we'll help spook 'em by taking some potshots at 'em from both sides. From what I've seen of them half-wild Mexican critters, it don't take much more'n a shadow to start 'em stampeding."

"Then they will break the wire!"

"That's the risk we'll have to take. But I don't figure they can break it all that easy. And you got to remember them steers never have run into a fence before."

"But if they do break the wire?"

"Then we've made a bet and maybe lost it. But I'm gambling the wire'll hold, and them steers is going to run rubbing on it. I figure that once the barbs start scratching 'em it'll drive 'em crazy. They'll turn and bolt toward the riverbed. A lot of 'em's gonna break their legs, and most of them on the side where the canyon is will fall in it, and I'm betting most of them are gonna get their legs or their necks broken."

"Are you sure it will be as you say, Longarm?"

"Not Bible-swearing sure, but I seen a lot of steers when I was cowhanding. Once a herd of steers gets spooked, there's not enough wranglers in all of Arizona Territory to gather 'em and form 'em up again."

"What will we be doing?" Shawahawaki asked. "There are many men who will be against us."

"Why, one of us will take cover in the canyon and the other one can scooch down behind the bluff that drops to the riverbed."

"Barnes and his men will shoot at us when they see us."

"Sure. But they'll be in the open and we'll be forted up. It's sure lucky that one who took my Colt didn't get my rifle, too. I guess he would've, only it was in my saddle scabbard."

"How long do you think it will be before the steers get here?" Shawahawaki asked.

"Maybe a little after noon, so we got plenty of time to fill this hole and set up the ends of the barbwire. Then all we got to do is wait for them fellows to get here."

Chapter 15

"We been waiting a long time, Shawahawaki, but if I ain't mistaken, I hear a few steers blatting," Longarm said.

"I have just heard them, too," the Papago agreed. "Now all we can do is wait and see if our fence is strong enough."

Longarm and Shawahawaki were hunkered down beside a low cliff fifty or sixty yards upriver from the fence, where a long rise in the ground offered a bit of shade from the overhead sun. They'd worked until mid-morning finishing their makeshift fence, and after eating a few bites from Longarm's trail rations both of them had been glad to settle down and rest while waiting for the outlaws to arrive.

"Should one of us stay awake to watch?" Shawahawaki had asked when Longarm stretched out and announced that he was going to take a nap while they waited.

"There ain't no need to. Barnes and his bunch have put in the morning shaping up their herd and chasing after strays and then driving up to however close they are to us now," Longarm had explained. "They likely won't get here any time soon. And a rest'll freshen us up. It just might give us the edge we need, because when them outlaws get here they're going to be as worn out as we were a little bit ago. We ain't got a thing to worry about."

In spite of Longarm's reassurance, when they had settled down to rest neither man had slept. They'd both closed their eyes, but the need to keep their ears cocked for the sounds of approaching cattle drove the thought of sleep from their minds. Both jumped to their feet when small distant noises reached their ears from the darkness, and after exchanging glances they nodded agreement that they'd arrived at the time when the final showdown with the renegades was very near.

"We'll just stay right here a little while longer," Longarm said at last, as the sounds of the approaching herd grew louder. "By now them steers are bound to be getting tired. Them half-wild critters are feisty enough as it is, and I'd guess that right about now they're hurting for water more'n a little bit. You start out to trail a bunch of wild Mexican steers like that, and you'll find out they got a way of being testy."

"Then you think we can scatter them?" Shawahawaki asked.

"I figure we got about as much chance as a greenhorn in a fixed poker game, and that ain't such a much. But like the man said, it's the only game in town."

They fell silent again and sat for a long time without speaking as they listened to the sounds of the outlaws' cattle herd growing steadily closer. At last Longarm stood up and told his companion, "I guess it's about time to split up now and get ready for 'em."

Shawahawaki got to his feet at once, and said, "I will try to remember what you have told me about the cattle, Longarm. I would be very sad if I made a mistake that could spoil our plan."

"You'll do fine," Longarm assured the Papago. "Just don't let yourself get buffaloed."

They mounted and set out. Shawahawaki turned his horse toward the dry canyon and Longarm headed for the river. He rode back up to the barbwire strand and sat looking at it for a long moment, feeling very exposed in the open country, with no trees or shrubs or rock formations where he could take shelter. The only place that offered even a small bit of concealment was the high wall of sandy soil that marked the old course of the river.

He pulled his mount as close to the wall's side as possible and dismounted. The top of the bluff hid his horse, and Longarm led the animal to its shelter. Then he hunkered down and lighted a cigar while he listened to the blatting of the approaching steers and the occasional shouts raised by their renegade drivers.

Only a few minutes went by before the dull thumping of the steers' hooves reached Longarm's ears as the herd grew closer and closer. He heard a steer's throaty angry snort, and then another of the animals loosed a similar huffing cry. Longarm stood up at once, stepped over to his horse and mounted, and now could see for a greater distance across the short stretch of barren desert that separated him from the herd.

A knot of cattle had formed at the strand of barbwire. The animals that had first run into the makeshift barrier were rearing and trying to turn away, but the pressure of those behind them made movement almost impossible. The cattle just behind the leaders of the herd kept moving forward. Their heads, which had been sagging in the desert's heat, were raising now as the squalls from those being cut by the barbwire grew louder.

Behind the knots of milling steers that were pushing

177

against the cruel cutting barbwire, three or four of the outlaws were slashing the steers with quirts or the loose ends of their reins, trying to reach the front of the herd through the animals that were now packed in a thick unyielding mass.

Though Longarm could see only a short distance beyond the cattle and riders that were at the fence, he could hear the voices of other men as well as the raucous blats of steers that were being crowded into the barbwire beyond his range of vision.

"Old son, that fence ain't going to stand up much longer," Longarm muttered as he reached for the rifle in his saddle scabbard. "Not with all that beef shoving into it!"

He'd barely finished speaking when the jam broke. The mass of steers behind those caught by the fence began turning aside. Some headed to the left along the fence line in the direction of Shawahawaki's position, others poured toward the rim of the precipitous drop to the old riverbed.

Now the stream of cattle rushing toward his position took all of Longarm's attention, though he was always aware of the movements of the riders trying to herd them. The air was filled with the noises of men shouting, cattle blatting, and an occasional shot from the area guarded by Shawahawaki.

When the steers that were breaking from the packed mass that pressed against the barbwire reached the drop-off to the old riverbed, those in the lead tried to stop. The pressure of the animals behind them was by now too great. The leaders plunged off the drop, their angry guttural cries turning into bleats of panic as they fell. Some landed headfirst on the sandy soil at the foot of the cliff, and in spite of the other noises, Longarm heard the loud snaps of their necks or legs breaking.

A few of the steers that did not die but had only the wind knocked out of them were in the riverbed by now. They began scattering as they struggled to their feet. Fifty yards beyond the fence Longarm saw the head and shoulders of one of the herdsmen appear in silhouette against the bright sky. He quickly dismounted and headed for cover.

For a moment the rider did not see Longarm, and when he did catch sight of him he dragged his rifle from its saddle scabbard and shouldered it, but Longarm had seen him first. His Winchester was already in his hands and moving to his shoulder. While the outlaw was still raising the muzzle of his rifle, Longarm's slug was singing its song of death as it whistled toward its target. The outlaw pitched out of his saddle. He landed at the base of the steep drop-off and lay motionless.

There had been no letup in the pressure of the main body of the herd against those trapped by the barbwire strand, and now the wire was showing signs of giving way. It was singing its protest against the strain against it in a shrill buzzing whine that rose above the flattened noises of thunking hooves, shouting men, neighing horses, and blatting cattle, but by now the shape of the herd was changing.

Finding their forward movement stopped by the mass of steers trapped against the barbwire, those further back in the herd were turning. The late arrivals hitting the motionless and immovable mass of cattle close to the fence were forced toward the drop-off into the old riverbed or toward the other end of the fence at the canyon. A constant parade of blatting, head-tossing cattle began flowing in both directions behind the compact immovable mass of the group that had stopped.

Still more turned away from the packed bulge at the fence and moved toward the canyon, where more shots told of the separate battle between Shawahawaki and the outlaws. Others veered off in the direction of the drop-off, its steep side rising sheer from the bed of the ancient river. These steers, like those before them, had no choice and no chance. They reached the ledge's edge and plunged down to the riverbed.

A few landed safely, but many more of them did not survive the fall. The lucky steers whose necks or legs or backs were not broken when they landed were beginning to wander across the wide expanse that led to the river. Longarm had started picking off with his rifle those which had not been crippled, when a shot cracked from the top of the bluff and the slug kicked up sand between the hooves of his horse.

Longarm looked up at the man on the bluff and saw that he was levering a fresh shell into the chamber of his gun. Swiveling where he stood, Longarm fired.

His aim was as accurate as before. The horseman sagged in his saddle, then toppled slowly out of it. His limp body fell to the edge of the cut and rolled down it to the riverbed, where it settled in a crumpled and motionless huddle beside the sprawled body of the man Longarm had shot earlier.

Longarm glanced up to see if any more immediate danger was threatening. He saw no outlaws, only the riderless horse of the man he'd just shot, and only a few scattered steers before a rise in the curving wall of the old riverbed cut off his view.

Returning to the face of the bluff, Longarm mounted and was turning his mount to the slant to ride up to the top of the riverbed when he suddenly twitched the reins and reversed his direction.

"You're getting too damn careless, old son," he chided himself as he started toward the two sprawled forms at the base of the drop-off. "One of them fellows there, or maybe both of 'em, might still be alive. The last thing you need right now is to get backshot."

As he drew closer to the forms of the men he'd shot, Longarm could see that he'd not needed to be concerned about the accuracy of his shooting. One of the men lay on his back, his eyes staring lifelessly into the cloudless sky. The other lay facedown in the same crumpled heap in which he'd landed after falling from the ledge.

Longarm was about to turn his horse when he saw the butt of a revolver protruding from the belt of the man who lay sprawled facedown on the sandy soil. It was a pistol butt he'd have recognized anywhere, that of his own Colt.

Dismounting, Longarm bent over the dead man and retrieved his weapon. He checked the cylinder to be sure the Colt was still fully loaded, found that it was, and restored it to his holster. Only then did he turn the dead man's body over, and when he did so he looked into the death-fixed eyes of Rusty Barnes. He stared at the dead man for a moment, then turned and walked slowly back to his horse. Mounting, he set out to rejoin Shawahawaki.

On the higher ground the blatting of the scattered cattle as well as the neighing of horses and the shouts of the outlaws had diminished. No more shots were coming from the direction of the canyon, and Longarm decided that Shawahawaki had also been successful in turning the cattle that had run in that direction. Twitching the reins of his horse, he turned the animal to ride parallel to the sagging strand of wire.

As Longarm rode in the direction of the canyon he

heard only distant yells from the retreating renegades and the occasional bawl of a confused steer. All along its length the wire of the improvised fence was sagging now. Its barbs were dark, glistening with fresh blood and tufted with furry fuzz from the hides of the steers that had been pushed into it.

Longarm had gone only a very short distance when he saw Shawahawaki riding to meet him. He reined in and waited. When the Papago was within earshot, Longarm called, "How does it look down there where you were?"

"There are many dead steers in the bottom of the canyon," the Papago said. "All the men are gone. I fired only a few shots when I saw one of them getting close, and he came no closer."

"Looks like our little pieces of barbwire did their job, then," Longarm went on. "There's a couple more dead men back there in the riverbed. One of 'em is that Barnes fellow that started all this ruckus. The others are all scattered out toward the ranch. From what I could see, they ain't even trying to get them Mexican steers formed up into a herd again, so it's dollars to doughnuts they'll just give up and go back to Mexico."

"And do you not think they will come back?"

"It ain't likely, with that Rusty Barnes fellow dead. Them others don't want land or cattle, they're just hired guns. So it looks like your wheat stalks are safe."

"Then we will go back to our mesa?"

"Sure. Even if we have to ride through the night."

"And you will stay with us a while? I am sure Aropi will say we must have a dance to celebrate and you will be our honored guest."

"Well, I'll tell you, Shawahawaki, I ain't much of a one for any kind of blowout," Longarm said. "If it's all

182

the same to you and Aropi, I'll just stop long enough to wish you well and say good-bye." A reminiscent smile tugged at the corners of his lips as he said, "You see, I got some unfinished business waiting for me back in Denver and I'm in a sorta hurry to get back there and take care of it."

Watch for

LONGARM AND THE MAD DOG KILLER

one hundred twenty-fourth novel in
the bold LONGARM series
from Jove

coming in April!